Dreams Adrift

(A River Dream Novel)

D W Davis

Published by River Sailor Literary

River Sailor Literary

Post Office Box 458

Pikeville, North Carolina 27863-0458, USA

ISBN:0983355657
ISBN-13: 978-0-9833556-5-6

ACKNOWLEDGMENTS

DREAMS ADRIFT brings my River Dream Trilogy to a close and as I bid adieu to Michael, Maeve, and Rhiannon I want to take a moment to acknowledge again my most ardent fan, my harshest critic, and my constant source of inspiration - my lovely wife Karen.

Karen, and our sons –Alex and Zack – have patiently (usually) and supportively acted as my proofreaders, sounding boards, and cheerleaders throughout the long process from the first draft of *RIVER DREAM* through the final edits of *DREAMS ADRIFT*. I could never have done this without them.

Every author needs an editor and I have been blessed with an awesome editor in my dear friend Jeanie Sherman. Thanks to her advice, support, and constructive criticism my readers have enjoyed much more entertaining books than I could have produced on my own.

And finally, to all the River Dreamers out there who have encouraged and supported me; thank you for helping me realize my personal River Dream.

Prologue

The grass strip at River Dream looked brown and forlorn through the wind screen of our new Cessna Skylane as I lined up to land. The wind sock showed a stiff wind out of the northwest. Northwest winds promised a cold weekend on the river. Maeve and I would be glad for the woodstove once I got a fire going and it started putting out its dry, comforting heat.

My preference would have been for a light north wind for my first attempt at landing the Cessna at River Dream. The fine folks at Cessna had assured me the landing gear on the Skylane was rugged enough for the twelve-hundred-foot grass runway at River Dream, and that the runway was plenty long enough to handle the Skylane.

The Cessna was a late Christmas present for Maeve. As attached as I was to my old Piper Cub, Maeve convinced me we needed something with a greater carrying capacity than the little two-seater could manage. The Skylane, while still being able to land at River Dream, could carry the two of us in the cockpit as well as two passengers and two hundred pounds of baggage. I found a good home for the Piper Cub at the Air and Space Museum.

Our first trip to River Dream in the Cessna would be the first of many cold, wet weekends at River Dream that rainy winter. Cold in Coastal Carolina may not be like the cold of a New England winter, and it has nothing on a cold day around the Great Lakes, but we were spoiled by the relatively mild winters with which our part of the world was normally graced. The chilly, damp, gray winter we endured between our October marriage and our June wedding was not the kind of winter to which Maeve and I were accustomed.

Our weekdays that winter and spring were consumed with class work, homework, wedding plans, and the details of daily life. We spent our weekends at River Dream recharging and rediscovering our passion for one another.

At long last, winter, like a reluctant stray resigning itself to the idea that it wasn't wanted, gradually gave way to the warmer days of spring. With its green leaves and scent of honeysuckle, it was the kind of spring that reminded folks why they loved living in the South.

Eventually, summer weather, if not technically summer itself, arrived in eastern North Carolina, and the date for our June wedding - eight months after our marriage at the Magistrate's office - drew close. When classes were done and the wedding was only a week away, Maeve and I decided we needed one more weekend at River Dream before the big event.

One

A crosswind set the grass on the landing strip swaying - reminding me it needed to be mowed - and buffeted the Cessna as I lined up for a landing at River Dream. We had one good bounce before I could keep all three wheels on the ground, and for a moment I feared we wouldn't stop before reaching the end of the runway. It wasn't one of my better landings. Maeve, who'd become a fair pilot herself, let me know it.

"Don't you know the old saying about landings?" I asked, after I breathed a sigh of relief.

"Which old saying would that be?" Maeve said, raising an eyebrow in my direction.

"Any landing you can walk away from is a good landing," I quipped as I climbed from the cockpit.

"Then I guess that qualifies as a good landing, barely," she said.

Using a lawn tractor, we towed the Cessna into its new hangar before climbing into the Jeep.

"It's a good thing we left the doors on," Maeve said as, on the short drive to the house, large drops of cold rain began to splatter on the hood, turning the dust on it to mud. Leaves left over from the fall were kicked up by the wind and stuck to the wet windshield. The weatherman had predicted a strong cold front moving in from New England overnight. Winds out of the northeast always made for interesting conditions along our stretch of the Neuse.

"I think we should check on the boats before we get comfortable inside," I said, "while it's still light."

Maeve glanced at the darkening sky. "That's a good idea. We'll get soaked, though."

I nodded. "Then I guess we'd better hurry."

We parked the Jeep and made our way carefully down the rain-slick dock to the boats. *Geddaway*, our twenty-six foot cruising sailboat, was up on the lift and looked secure. *Riverscape*, the nineteen-foot day sailor, needed some tightening up on the spring lines. The twenty-foot Grady-White fishing boat was riding fine.

Maeve was right. By the time we were done, we were soaked.

I smiled when I looked at Maeve in the fading light. "We'd better get inside," I said. "I'll put some water on for tea while you dry off and change."

"Good idea, Mike," Maeve said, running her fingers through her wet hair.

When we got to the porch, it took me a moment to dig the house key out of the pocket of my soaked jeans.

Maeve pressed herself against me, shivering. "It's a good thing we're not expecting company," she said.

I finally got the key in my hand and opened the door. We hurried inside. The house was still warm from the heat of the day but would cool quickly as the rain and wind pulled the heat away. I hurried to the kitchen and filled the copper tea kettle. Maeve headed straight for the bedroom to change into dry clothes. After lighting the burner under the kettle, I went to the living room and started a fire in the wood stove.

"What's the matter?" Maeve asked. She was wrapped in her fluffy pink terrycloth robe, a matching towel around her neck. "You're not cold, are you?"

"I'm not cold, sweetheart," I responded, smiling at her over my shoulder, hoping she couldn't hear my teeth chattering, "but I thought you might be chilly."

"You're so thoughtful, Michael," she said with a smirk. She pulled the lapels of the robe closed and shuddered. "Actually, I was starting to feel cold."

Looking at Maeve in her robe, her wet hair plastered down on her head, I couldn't get over how beautiful she looked even so.

"Michael," Maeve said, a light blush coloring her cheeks. "I must look awful."

"No," I said, as I stood up and reached out to take her hand, "you look beautiful to me. You always look beautiful to me, Maeve."

A shy smile lit her face as I took her in my arms. Just as my lips covered hers, the tea kettle whistled.

"I need to get that," Maeve said.

"It'll wait," I told her.

I held her to me, pressing my lips once more to hers. The tea kettle whistle intensified in counterpoint to the rising passion of our kiss.

When, at last, we parted to draw breath, Maeve pushed me away playfully and said, "I really need to take care of the kettle before it burns up."

Reluctant to release her, I replied, "Hurry back. I'm burning up, too, and need to be taken care of."

Maeve smiled, kissed me quickly, and sashayed out of the living room toward the kitchen, her robe swirling about her, giving me an enticing glimpse of her trim, toned legs.

The rain continued through the night and all day Saturday, finally blowing on out to sea in the wee hours of Sunday morning. Maeve and I spent the time enjoying having nowhere to go and nowhere to be. When Sunday dawned cool, clear, and relatively calm, we decided to sail *Riverscape* to Oriental for lunch at the Wharf. We called my folks to let them know we'd decided to stay home another night and would fly back to Wilmington Monday morning.

My mother was not happy to hear about our change in plans. "What about final arrangements for the wedding?" she asked.

"There's nothing that can't wait until we get home Monday," I told her. There weren't any arrangements that hadn't already been checked and double checked that I knew of.

It was a short walk from the Wharf to the market. I was in the mood to grill some steaks for supper. Maeve agreed, and we picked up the fixings for steak, corn on the cob, and baked potatoes. The market had some fresh-baked apple pies, so we added one of those and some ice cream to our list. At the last minute, we remembered to get some ice for the cooler on *Riverscape*. The ice cream wouldn't have made it far otherwise.

Theresa, the girl working at the register, smiled when she saw our choices.

"It looks like someone's planning to grill out," she said. "At least the weather's nice enough for it today."

Smiling as she slid her arm around my waist, Maeve replied, "Oh, I don't know. We haven't minded the rain."

Theresa gave Maeve a knowing look. "I know what you mean. Sometimes it's nice to be stuck at home with nothing to do."

The wind had moved from the northwest to almost directly west as we headed back to River Dream. We were able to make good time on a close reach, only having to tack once before dropping sail and motoring the last little way to the dock.

I walked out onto the back porch to get the grill going and realized I didn't know if we had any charcoal. Fortunately, we did, just enough to cook the steaks. While I was busy cleaning the grill, Maeve put the potatoes in the oven and then came out back to shuck the corn.

Watching her brush the silks off the corn, I asked, "Do you know how happy I am being your man?"

She stopped and looked up at me. "If you're half as happy being my man as I am being your wife, then yes, Michael, I know how happy you are." She smiled and went back to shucking the corn. "What brought that on?"

Picking up the grill I'd been cleaning to get a better look at it, I said, "This weekend did, I guess. I think I'll always remember this weekend in a special way."

Maeve turned that lovely smile on me. "I think you're right, Mike. But we'll have years and years of weekends like this."

"I know," I said, satisfied the grill was as clean as I could get it. "But somehow I think this one will be *that* weekend."

Maeve nodded her understanding and announced she'd finished shucking the corn. "I guess I'll wait to start this," she said. "Those potatoes will take a while."

Setting down the bag of charcoal I'd just picked up, I said, "Then I won't start the grill just yet. What should we do in the meantime?"

Maeve took my hand and looked toward the house.

"Sweetheart," I said, "I love how you think."

We did get around to grilling those steaks and enjoyed a

nice supper over in the screened room, by the river. After dinner we sat in the swing. Maeve reminded me of the first time we spent an evening together in that screened room.

"I helped you come up with the name for *Riverscape*, remember?"

"Oh yes, I remember."

"Do you remember what I said to you after we'd come up with the name?" she asked coyly.

"Trust me sweetheart, I haven't forgotten."

Maeve turned her head up and said, "Then are you going to kiss me, or what?"

Very gently, I slid my hand behind her head, the softness of her hair caressing the skin on my hand, and leaned forward, covering her lips with mine.

The next morning we got up, cleaned the house, double checked the boats, and headed back to Wrightsville Beach. There were still some final preparations for the wedding we had to take care of.

Two

With the wedding only two days away, I went to the Wright Isle Resort, at Maeve's insistence, to make sure no last-minute details had been overlooked.

"Michael," Hernando said as we walked back to the hotel from the spot on the beach where the ceremony would take place, "everything is ready for your special day. I have overseen the preparations myself. It will be wonderful. You have my word."

"I know you'll take good care of us, Hernando," I said. He was an excellent resort manager. "But you understand, Maeve sent me to check one more time."

"I think, Michael," Hernando said with a grin, "perhaps she wanted you out of her hair more than she was worried about the arrangements here."

"I'd agree with that," I said. We shared a laugh. "Hernando, I'll let you get back to work."

"I'm looking very forward to Saturday, Michael," Hernando said before turning to go back to his office.

As I walked across the lobby on my way out, I was stopped cold by a voice softly calling my name. A chill ran down my spine as I turned around.

"Hello, Michael," Rhiannon said softly.

My chest tightened until drawing a breath took conscious effort. I felt at once chilled and as if the lobby was suddenly too warm. I stood there, wide-eyed, dumb-struck, trying to take in the fact that Rhiannon was standing there in front of me. She was even more beautiful than I remembered. The question running through my mind was *why is she here now?*

"Are you surprised to see me?" Rhiannon asked hesitantly, taking a step towards me.

Finding my voice, I said, my tone cold as dry ice, "I am surprised to see you. I honestly never expected to see you again."

"My folks told me you were getting married. I dropped everything to get here. You wouldn't believe what I had to go through. I couldn't believe you were getting married, Michael," Rhiannon said. She took another step.

We'd sent an invitation to her parents. They'd known me all my life. They were close friends of my parents. Of course we invited them. Then another thought hit me, *Doesn't she know we're already married?*

Then I thought, *My getting married was enough to get her to come home, but my clinging to life in a hospital bed wasn't.*

"Aren't you glad to see me?" she asked quietly, moving another step closer.

Was I glad? No. The chill that had come over me on first seeing her was being burned out by the heat of long-suppressed anger. I strained to keep my voice even. "Why did you come now?"

The acid tone in my voice stopped her. She was close enough that I could see the tears brimming in her eyes.

"I've missed you, Michael. I've missed you so much."

"Then why wait until now to come back?" I snapped at

her, unable to bridle my anger.

"Michael…" Rhiannon started.

"Where were you all those months I was in the hospital? Where were you all that time I was in rehab learning to walk again?"

"Michael, I'm sorry. I'm so sorry I wasn't there," Rhiannon said, tears starting to run down her face.

"Yeah, I'm sorry too. I'm sorry for all those hours I spent waiting for you to come, just knowing in my heart that the next person to walk into that room would be my Rhiannon. But my Rhiannon never came. She had something more important to do than be with me."

"Michael, I wanted to come, but I couldn't. Those people needed me. I was doing important work."

"It was more important for you to be one more volunteer digging a well in some God-forsaken country than to be there for me when I needed you most," I said. I could see how my bitterness hurt her, and I didn't care.

"Michael, I'm sorry, I made a mistake. How many times must I say I'm sorry?" She was sobbing.

My face became a cold mask. "You never have to say it again, Rhiannon. It's too late for that now."

She choked off the sobs and challenged me. "You want me to believe you don't love me anymore? I don't believe it."

"The Rhiannon I grew up with, that Rhiannon I will always love. The Rhiannon I waited and waited for, who never came, to whom I wasn't as important as a bunch of strangers a continent away - I have no feelings for her."

"You told me once you'd wait for me until the day after forever, no matter what," Rhiannon said, tears flowing from her eyes again.

"I was in that hospital forever, Rhiannon. And the day after forever, when I finally walked out of that place, you…weren't…there. Good-bye, Rhiannon." I turned and walked away.

Behind me, Rhiannon spoke. She spoke one last apology, and a pledge.

"Michael, I am sorry. I promise you this: If ever the day comes when you need your Rhiannon again, I will not fail you. I will be there then. Michael, I promise."

I stopped, took a deep breath, and turned around, but she was gone. I stood there looking at the spot where she'd been standing for I don't know how long.

Finally, I walked out to my car and drove to the north end of the island. As I got out and unlocked the gate, I heard a car pull up behind me. My heart leaped in my chest and tears filled my eyes when I turned and saw Maeve's Porsche. I looked to heaven and said a silent "Thank you" to God.

Maeve jumped out of her car and rushed over to me, eyes wide with concern.

"Michael, what's wrong? I saw you drive right by our street. You didn't even see me. Michael, what is it? Is something wrong?"

"Not anymore," I said, taking her in my arms. "Just let me hold you. Maeve, I love you so much. You do know that, don't you?"

Maeve pressed her head against my chest and tightened her arms around me. "I know, Michael, I know. I love you, too, baby, I love you."

I kissed her, took her by the hand, and led her through the gate into the unspoiled dunes of the reserve.

"Where are we going, Michael?"

"We're going away from everything and everyone. Things have been too hectic these last couple of days. There's been so much going on. I just need to be with you and only you, just for a few precious moments."

Maeve clung tightly to my hand as we climbed the dune. At the top we stopped, sat, and watched the waves roll in under a cloudless blue sky.

"On a clear day like this, you feel like you can see to the other side," I said.

I put my arm around Maeve. She snuggled her head against my shoulder and didn't say anything. I wanted to tell her about Rhiannon, but I wasn't sure how. At last, I just told her.

"Maeve, Rhiannon was at the Wright Isle Resort when I went to see Hernando."

"I knew she was in town, Michael," Maeve said. After a moment's pause, she continued. "Your mother called to say she'd stopped by their house looking for you."

"Oh," I said. My shoulders slumped and I looked down at the sand. "I didn't know that."

We sat quietly for what seemed like a long time. Waves broke on the shore with a hypnotic rhythm. The sea oats around us rustled in the wind. A lone gull circled overhead, hoping we might offer up a scrap of something. He dipped his wings and, with an indignant screech, turned his attention south.

Maeve raised her head, her lip pulled tight between her teeth. "What…" she started to ask. She took a deep breath before trying again. "What did she want?"

I took a moment to decide how to answer. "I guess she wanted to tell me she was sorry."

Maeve sat quietly for several minutes. I wondered if she guessed what Rhiannon was sorry for - for not coming home when I needed her. Before I decided I should explain, she asked, "What did you say?"

"I told her I was sorry, too," I said. "Sorry I ever thought she and I had a future."

"Oh," Maeve said. Again the quiet settled over us, the only sounds the whisper of the wind through the sea oats and the crash of the waves on the shore.

I sighed deeply. "Then she asked me if I still loved her."

Maeve stiffened and then forced herself to relax against me. "What did you say to that?"

"I told her the truth," I said.

"And what was that?" Maeve asked. Her voice trembled as if she was afraid to hear the answer.

"I told her no," I said, turning to face the woman I loved. "I love you, Maeve. I want to spend the rest of my life with you. I want to share all my triumphs and tribulations with you. I want to share my joys with you, and I want to make you happy. There is only you, Maeve. She was my childhood sweetheart. You are the love of my life."

Maeve's response was a kiss. A kiss that said all that needed to be said between us. It was a kiss that told me how much she loved me, how much my love meant to her, and how much she loved being mine.

My response showed her that she was the only love in my life, the only woman I wanted to be with, and the only person I desired to share the rest of my life with. We kissed, and then we held each other as the sun set behind us and night settled on the ocean.

Maeve's sister Cynthia was waiting for us when we got to the house. "Where have you two been?" she wanted to know.

Maeve batted her heather blue eyes and smiled an angelic smile. "We've been spending some quality time together with the dunes."

Leaving Cynthia to figure that out, we walked past her to our room.

Three

Two days later, under a cobalt blue sky dotted with snow white cumulus clouds, I stood with my best man, Hans, at the temporary altar erected on the beach in front of the Wright Isle Resort. First Maeve's parents, and then my parents, were escorted down the aisle and seated. All heads turned back toward the resort when the organist began to play *Canon in D* by Pachelbel.

Chase appeared at the top of the walkway, flanked by Kim and Malori. The ladies were stunning in their cornflower blue tea-length gowns. Chase's tux, light tan with a cornflower blue cummerbund, matched them perfectly. If Derrick hadn't left for Parris Island the month before, he would have been Kim's escort. Chase didn't seem to mind escorting those two lovely ladies down the aisle. The ring bearer and flower girl were next.

As Maeve and I had no nieces or nephews of our own for the roles, we'd invited Alfredo Dupree's twin grandchildren to take part in the wedding. They were absolutely adorable. Isadora's dress was a perfect copy of the bridesmaid dresses, and little Alfred's tux was a miniature of the ones Chase and

Hans wore. Alfred walked so proudly, holding his little pillow with the decorative rings practically up to his chin. Isadora walked shyly beside her brother, gently spreading the rose petals along the wooden walk.

Then it was Cynthia's turn. Her dress was a shade lighter than the bridesmaids' and her bouquet a bit fuller. Hans' cummerbund was the same blue as Cynthia's dress. She stood tall at the top of the walkway and looked towards me. Even at that distance I could tell tears were filling her eyes. A smile formed and, taking a breath, she began her trek down the aisle. As she took her place on the bride's side of the altar, the music changed.

As Clark's "Trumpet Voluntary" began playing, Maeve and her father appeared at the top of the walkway leading to the beach. With each step they took I could feel my pulse beating faster. Maeve looked so beautiful in her wedding dress, a tea-length white gown with hints of yellow along the frill. Her bouquet was white orchids. White sandals adorned her feet. She wore the pearl choker her mother had worn at her wedding. Her veil was held on by a ring of small white flowers. The veil was thin, and I could see Maeve's smile beaming as they came down the aisle. My heart swelled with love for her. My white tux, with a yellow cummerbund, complimented her dress perfectly.

Due to the unique circumstances of our wedding, being that it followed our marriage by several months, Maeve and I, with the help of the preacher and other interested parties, had made some changes to the wedding ceremony. As her father walked her to the altar, I stepped down to take her hand from him, and she joined me before the preacher.

Reverend McIntyre addressed our guests. "Who supports this couple as they affirm their vows this day?"

My parents and Maeve's folks were supposed to say "We

do." Instead, a chorus of "we do's" came from our parents, the wedding party, and most of the guests. I looked aside at Maeve. She was looking at me with the same questioning look. The preacher was smiling a conspiratorial smile. Evidently, someone made plans of their own. We wondered what other surprises might await us.

Reverend McIntyre continued the ceremony. "Friends and family of the couple, we have gathered here this beautiful morning to be with Michael and Maeve as they affirm before God and this company their vows of marriage. They have come together as husband and wife, devoted to each other in love, to confirm their wish and intent to remain together in the bonds of matrimony as long as they both shall live."

The preacher then nodded to Rick, who'd been my boat skipper in the Navy. He'd gladly accepted the assignment when we asked him to read a passage from the "Song of Solomon."

"My love spoke and said to me, arise my darling, my beautiful one, and come with me. See, the winter is past, the rain is over and gone. The flowers have appeared in the fields; the season of singing has come, and the cooing of doves is heard in our land. The fig tree has ripened its figs, and the blossoming vines spread their fragrance. Arise my darling, my beautiful one, and come with me."

After he returned to his seat, Reverend McIntyre addressed the guests once more.

"Marriage is not a covenant to be entered into lightly. Michael and Maeve pledged their lives and love to each other forever more. Today, in the presence of God, their families, and their friends, they will make new their vows."

Maeve and I had given a lot of thought to our vows. When we were married in the magistrate's office, we'd taken the standard wedding vows, but for our wedding we had written very special vows to exchange.

Reverend McIntyre turned to me and said softly, "Michael, please say your vow to Maeve."

Maeve and I turned to face each other. Tears filled my eyes as I looked into hers, and I felt the love flowing between us like a current. Swallowing hard against my emotions, I spoke my vow to Maeve.

"Maeve, my love, my life, I promise you this day all my love, my loyalty, my laughter, my mind, and my heart. All that I have and all that I am are yours today and forever. I will be your friend, your lover, your confidant; the father of your children, your strength when you tire, your warmth when you are cold, your shelter in the storm, the one who will stand by you through all things."

I stopped and turned to Hans, who handed me the new ring I would place on Maeve's finger.

"I give you this ring as a symbol of our unending love and unity."

I slid the ring on her finger next to the one she'd worn since that day in the magistrate's office.

"From this day forward we will walk together as one."

Maeve squeezed my hands tight and spoke her vow to me.

"Michael, my love, my life, I promise you this day all my love, my loyalty, my laughter, my mind, and my heart. All that I have and all that I am are yours today and forever. I will be your friend, your lover, your confidant; the mother of your children, your strength when you tire, your warmth when you are cold, your shelter in the storm, the one who will stand by you through all things."

Maeve turned to Cynthia, her maid of honor, and took the new ring she would place on my finger.

"I give you this ring as a symbol of our unending love and unity. From this day forward we will walk together as one."

The preacher nodded to Beth, whose beautiful soprano voice soon filled the air with the words of "There is Love." While she sang, Maeve and I stood looking into each others' eyes. I know the smile on my face matched the one on hers.

As the final notes of the song were carried away on the morning breeze, Reverend McIntyre once again addressed our guests.

"Michael and Maeve, as you have affirmed your vows of matrimony here before God and this company, I ask that the Lord's blessing be upon your union." Then he smiled at me and said, "Michael, you may kiss your bride."

I reached up gently and lifted Maeve's veil. Then we kissed a kiss that would be talked about by our family and friends for years to come. It surpassed the kiss we'd shared on the wildlife pier the night I proposed, even the kiss we'd shared that night on the dune. I don't know how long it might have gone on if the preacher hadn't coughed politely to remind us we weren't exactly alone on the beach. Maeve and I giggled as we moved apart and turned towards our guests.

"Ladies and gentlemen, family and friends," intoned Reverend McIntyre, "Michael and Maeve Lanier."

With radiant smiles on our faces, we received the applause of our guests. The applause faded and we waited for the organist to begin playing the recessional. We'd picked "Jesu, Joy of Man's Desiring" by Bach. At the first strains of organ music Beth stood with her flute and, accompanied by several of our musically inclined friends, joined the organist in playing the song. Maeve and I looked at each other and laughed before walking up the aisle and across the wooden walkway to the resort's patio area where our wedding party joined us to form a receiving line.

As the guests filed past, they were shown into the banquet room where the reception luncheon would take place. The band was already set up and began playing background music as people started to fill the room. Maeve, her bridesmaids, my groomsmen, and I still had pictures to take. After the last of the guests filed past, Maeve reached up and turned my head to face her.

"Well, Mr. Lanier, I think that went well."

"Yes, Mrs. Lanier, I think it did," I said.

"This may sound funny, Michael," Maeve said as we made our way back toward the beach for pictures, "but I now feel like we're Married with a capital M. Do you know what I mean?"

Now that she'd put it that way, I realized she'd described perfectly the feeling I was feeling. "I hadn't thought of it like that, but I think you're right."

Maeve smiled and hugged me.

It seemed to take forever to get all the pictures taken, but at long last the photographer announced we were done. Relieved, we made our way to the banquet room. Maeve and I had to wait until our bridesmaids and groomsmen had taken their places at the head table so that we could be announced.

The clanking of glasses began as soon as we reached our seats. I wasn't sure if Hans or Chase started it, or perhaps it was Cynthia. Regardless, Maeve and I gave in with a quick kiss. The serving staff was filling glasses in preparation for the toasts. We would be toasted by both the Best Man and the Maid of Honor.

Always the gentleman, Hans insisted Cynthia go first. One of the staff brought her a microphone. She stood and raised her glass.

"As her big sister, I've known Maeve all her life."

Cynthia paused to let the expected chuckles die down.

"She was the typical annoying little sister, but she did have her good points. She's grown into a fine young lady and was blessed to find a fine young man like Michael to fall in love with. Sis, when you first brought him home I wasn't sure he was the guy for you, but seeing you two together, now I have no doubts. I wish you love and happiness through all your days."

She raised her glass high, "To Maeve and Michael."

"To Maeve and Michael," echoed through the room. Maeve and I both rose to our feet and embraced Cynthia. We were all in tears.

Then it was Hans' turn. He looked at Cynthia, Maeve, me, and finally back at Cynthia. She handed him the microphone.

"That is going to be a hard act to follow," he said quietly, for our ears only. Taking a deep breath, he picked up his glass and stood.

"I haven't known Michael quite all his life; it just feels that way," he started, earning his share of laughs. "We've been friends since as far back as I can remember. He is closer to me than a brother. They say you cannot pick your family, but you do get to pick your friends. Michael is the kind of friend I would pick to be family."

I felt tears welling again.

"I remember the first time Michael told me about Maeve. That was many years ago. I could see in his eyes and hear in his voice that there was something special about her, something that touched a place in his heart."

I remembered telling Hans about Maeve but hadn't realized I'd given him that impression.

"Last fall when he found her again, I saw that look in his

eyes and heard that something in his voice that had been missing all those years in between. I believe it was because he'd rediscovered his soul mate. There is love and then there is LOVE." He put special emphasis on the second love.

"May Michael and Maeve always know LOVE between them, and may they always be happy together."

He raised his glass high, "Here's to Michael and Maeve, long life and good times."

Once again, "To Michael and Maeve," echoed around the room.

Maeve and I rose to embrace Hans.

"That was beautiful, Hans," Maeve said through her tears. "I never knew that."

Hans, his hands gently upon her shoulders, said, "You never knew what?"

Maeve sniffed and said, "What you said about Michael, from when we first met. I didn't know about that."

Hans smiled and nodded.

We no sooner sat down than it was announced lunch was served. During the planning it was debated among the ladies involved whether to go with plated meals or a buffet. Offering my two cents worth, I'd expressed a preference for a buffet. Much to my surprise, that's what we wound up doing.

The kitchen staff outdid themselves preparing the buffet. They'd included a little something for everyone. Chicken, beef, pork, seafood, and a selection of vegetarian items all adorned the tables. Salads of every description, vegetables, diced fruits, and potatoes prepared in ways I could never have imagined complemented the main courses. There were soups and chowders. There was certainly no reason for anyone to leave that party hungry.

Maeve and I got to make the first pass at the buffet so we could eat our lunch and then mingle with our guests while they ate theirs. This allowed me to meet some of Maeve's family, aunts and uncles and such, and her to meet some of mine we probably wouldn't have otherwise.

As lunch began to wind down, we made our way back to the head table. Again, glasses were clanked and again we responded with a kiss, though it was hard to kiss while we were giggling.

With lunch done it was time for dessert. That meant cutting the cake. Our wedding cake was a beautiful four-layer cake. Each layer was separated by columns, making it look even bigger than it was. Rather than little bride and groom characters, our cake top was a blown glass heart encompassing two crystal swans.

As we approached the cake for the cutting, I reminded Maeve, "We're going to keep this dignified. No smooshing cake in my face, right?"

Maeve gave me a look of utter innocence. "Who, me?"

I knew I was in trouble.

The band broke into a rendition of "the bride feeds the groom," as the first piece was cut from the cake. The photographer made sure she had a good angle for the shot. Maeve carefully picked up the piece of cake, carefully held it up to my mouth, and as I carefully took a bite, she cheerfully mashed it onto my nose.

Her laughter turned to a look of concern when she saw the evil smile of intent on my face. The band changed the words to "the groom feeds the bride," as I sliced a piece of cake, carefully picked it up, carefully held it to Maeve's now nervous lips and waited for her to take a bite.

She hesitated just an instant and then lunged quickly, hoping to forestall any payback I might have in mind by gobbling up the whole piece before I could carry out my vengeance. Having expected that, I moved the cake down ever so slightly and she plunged her chin right into the frosting.

Her dark laugh made me just a bit nervous as she used her hand to wipe the frosting from her chin. I gingerly held out what was left of the cake to her and she bit it from my hand. Then, with a triumphant look, she wiped the frosting in her hand on my cheek.

Knowing she'd gotten in the last word, so to speak, I handed her a napkin to clean her hand, took one for myself to clean my face, and we were soon frosting free.

It was a good thing we cleaned up quickly because it was time to start the dances. For our dance we chose "She's Got a Way" by Billy Joel. That song always made me think of Maeve.

Maeve and Ted danced to "Through the Years" by Kenny Rogers for their father-daughter dance. There wasn't a dry eye in the house when they finished.

My mother chose Rod Stewart's "Have I Told You Lately" for us to dance to. My mom was an excellent dancer. I was glad for the lessons I'd taken in high school. After the mother-son dance the floor was opened up to anyone who wanted to join in the fun.

The band finished their first set, and it was time for throwing the bouquet. A cheer went up at this announcement, and the single ladies - including Kim, Cynthia, my cousin Denise, several of Maeve's friends from school, and my little sister Malori - jockeyed for position on the dance floor. I wasn't sure Malori should be included - she was barely twelve - but Maeve insisted.

Everyone cheered when Kim caught the bouquet. I was secretly relieved. It would have put a damper on the throwing of the garter had Malori been the lucky lady.

The single men, including Hans and Chase, then

crowded close to see who would catch the garter. Maeve's cousin, Paul, who was home from the Army on leave, won the contest. Paul was on his way from Fort Lewis, Washington, to a twelve-month tour in Korea.

Kim smiled coyly at Paul when he proudly showed her the garter. Maeve put her arm around Kim's shoulder and whispered something in her ear. Kim's eyes flew wide open in shock, and she turned a scandalized look on Maeve. I could only imagine what Maeve said to her, but Kim and Paul had danced several times, so I had a pretty good idea.

Chase grabbed a chair from a nearby table and placed it in the middle of the dance floor. Kim was escorted to the chair by the other single ladies. She sat down and crossed her legs demurely.

Paul, clasping his hands over his head like a victorious prize fighter, joined her at center stage. He took a knee at Kim's feet, slowly removed her shoe, and slid the garter over her foot and up to her ankle.

Pointing with his hands at the position of the garter, Paul looked at the other single guys with a raised eyebrow.

"Higher," they urged. "Higher."

Paul moved the garter slowly up Kim's calf and stopped just below her knee. Again, he pointed to the garter.

"Higher, higher."

Paul leered at Kim. She smiled back but didn't say no. He slowly moved the garter past her knee and began to slide it up her slender thigh. About three inches past her knee, Kim reached down and stopped him. Paul frowned, but Kim shook her head decisively *no*.

A chorus of good-natured booing ensued from the men while the ladies laughed. Paul replaced Kim's shoe, stood, and helped her to her feet. She kissed his cheek, and they hugged.

Our final act before leaving on our honeymoon was to

thank our guests. Then it was up to our room, a room we had reserved solely for this purpose, to change into our traveling clothes before making our way to the airport where the Cessna Skyline, fully loaded with the luggage we would need for our honeymoon, awaited us. It was a short flight to Raleigh. After we confirmed arrangements for storing the Cessna while we were gone, we caught a cab to the nearby Hilton. We spent our wedding night in their finest suite.

What Maeve and I hadn't known was that there had been one inconspicuous uninvited guest at our wedding. She didn't sit in the congregation, nor join us at the reception, but Rhiannon had watched the ceremony from her beach-front room on the fourth floor. As we disappeared into the reception, she'd said aloud to herself, "I wish you much happiness, Michael. I'm sorry that you didn't find it with me. I will keep my promise to you Michael; if you ever need me, I will be there for you." She closed the shade, picked up her suitcase, and being careful to avoid the reception, left the hotel, Wrightsville Beach, and the man she loved behind.

Four

Maeve and I rose late the next morning. Our flight out wasn't until mid-afternoon, so we were in no hurry. The dining room at the Hilton offered a lavish breakfast buffet, including a station where a talented young chef made a show out of preparing omelets to order.

Seeing how much the exuberant fellow loved working with the ingredients, I told Maeve, "I think I'll have a western omelet with the works."

Maeve wrinkled her nose. "I'll stick to my ham and cheese omelet, thank you very much."

Besides the omelets, the buffet included Belgian waffles, pancakes, biscuits with or without saw mill gravy, scrambled eggs, sausage links, bacon, several flavors of fruit juices, and some decent brews of coffee. The only thing lacking was genuine maple syrup. Everything else we tried was so good Maeve and I decided we could forgive the hotel for that.

After breakfast we returned to our room to repack our bags, check that we had our passports and plane tickets handy, and go over our flight itinerary. Then Maeve looked at me and asked, "What do you want to do until it's time to leave for the airport?"

My grin and the look in my eyes let her know what I was thinking we could do to pass the time.

"Michael," Maeve said, trying to sound scandalized. But she walked over, put her arms around my waist, and pulled me toward the bed.

We barely made it to checkout at eleven. I called the concierge from the room before we headed to the elevator, and she had a cab waiting to whisk us to the airport.

After checking our bags and getting our boarding passes, we had time for a leisurely lunch.

"Did you save room for dessert?" our server, Stephanie, asked after clearing away our lunch dishes.

I looked at Maeve, and said, "I don't know about you, but I'm going to try the marble cheesecake."

After gnawing at her lower lip for a moment, Maeve smiled and said, "We are on our honeymoon, after all. I'll have the chocolate mousse."

We enjoyed our desserts and then spent the rest of the time before our flight in front of the big plate-glass windows watching the planes take off and land.

"Airports are really cool places, Mike," Maeve commented. "They're full of people coming and going to all sorts of destinations around the world. There's a sense of adventure just being in an airport, don't you think? It's all very exciting."

"Whenever I see a plane take off I wonder about the people on board," I told her, gesturing towards a Boeing 727 starting down the runway. "I try to imagine where they're going and why, who they're leaving behind, and who they're going to see. Will they find what they're after or come back empty-handed, if they come back at all?"

The expression on Maeve's face told me she was trying to

imagine those things. Then her expression changed and she turned to me. "What about the planes landing? What do they make you think about?"

"When I see a plane land, I think about coming home. A landing plane always makes me think the people on board are returning from somewhere even though I know many probably aren't from here. I don't know why I think that. That's just how it feels."

We lost track of time while watching all those arrivals and departures, so we were caught by surprise when the attendant at the gate called for our flight to start boarding. Maeve and I grabbed our carry-on bags and got in line. The attendant checked our boarding passes and passports, smiled graciously, and wished us a pleasant flight.

We went out the door, down a flight of stairs, across the tarmac, up the boarding ladder, and into the plane. Our adventure had begun in earnest, and a few minutes later, as the pilot revved the engines and we started to taxi toward the runway threshold, we were truly on our way.

We changed planes at JFK and boarded our flight for Madrid. Eight hours later we landed in Spain. One last hop and we were in Gibraltar. We'd spent eleven hours on one plane or another and four more hours waiting around airports for flights.

Maeve and I were exhausted. Our bodies thought it was morning when in fact it was lunch time where we were.

"I think we should grab a bite to eat and then check into our hotel for a nap," Maeve suggested. I heartily agreed.

There was a quaint little bistro near our hotel, so we stopped there for some lunch before settling into our room for a nap. After waking up only long enough to enjoy dinner in the hotel's restaurant, we went back to our room and slept off the lingering effects of our flight.

A night of rest left us in good spirits as Maeve and I headed for the marina the next day. We boarded our chartered forty-one-foot sailboat and spent a day on the bay learning her ins and outs. The next morning just after sunup, fully provisioned and provided with the charts and paperwork we would need for our voyage, we left port. It was June 27.

We docked the first night at a marina near Sabinillas. Not wanting to miss the experience of Sabinillas' Friday Street Market, we'd arranged our sailing schedule to allow for a couple of days there. Sabinillas had a wonderful small-town feel, and we were tempted to stay longer, but the sea beckoned us onward.

Our second port of call was Marbella. Marbella was quite a change from the quiet little town of Sabinillas. After enjoying the sites and nightlife in Marbella, we sailed on to Fuengirola. In Fuengirola we enjoyed a visit to the zoo and Sohail Castle.

At our third port of call, Malaga, we finally spent a few nights away from the boat. Leaving the boat in Malaga, Maeve and I traveled inland about fifteen miles, or twenty-five kilometers to be metric about it, to a horse-riding resort in Alora, where we spent a few days riding the beautiful hills of Andalusia. The cabin we stayed in was somewhat austere but comfortable.

"They remind me of the cabins at a KOA campground back home," Maeve commented.

The horses were not Andalusian stallions. Instead I rode an Anglo-Arabian gelding while Maeve's mount was a Thoroughbred mare. We spent a couple of days working with the horses before going on an overnight trail ride into the highlands.

Around the campfire that night Maeve confessed to me. "Michael, you know I love sailing with you but, really, I think this has been my favorite part of our trip."

As much as I loved sailing, I had to admit it was pretty nice being off in the wilds of central Spain, camping out with my true love.

"I never knew you were so into horseback riding," I told Maeve.

"I used to ride a lot when I was younger. My Aunt Nancy, my mother's sister, paid for me to take riding lessons at day camp before I started going to Camp Riversail."

She leaned back and put her head on my shoulder. Looking up into the night sky, she said, "There are so many stars out tonight. Isn't it beautiful?"

I joined her in admiring the stars and with a slight twinge realized I couldn't recognize Star Jillian in that Spanish night sky.

"It is beautiful. For some reason I never thought European skies could be so dark and clear."

Maeve laughed. "Out here we're miles from any city lights. It's almost like being out in the middle of the sound at night. The stars shine through in all their glory."

Our ride the next day took us through some beautiful country. All too soon it seemed our days on horseback came to a close and we were in a taxi on our way back to Malaga.

Leaving Malaga, after restocking our provisions, we sailed the longest single stretch of our voyage to date, reaching Almunecar just as dusk was falling. It was a little tricky picking up the mooring buoy, but we made it on the second try, thanks to some helpful advice from a neighboring boat. Thanking him profusely for his help, we made fast and then invited him and his mate to come over for a visit.

A short time later Dwayne Stevens and his wife Joan were climbing aboard from their dinghy. They were fellow Americans taking a holiday cruise from Cartegena to

Gibraltar.

"We always take these two weeks and charter a boat somewhere far from home," Dwayne told us.

The Stevens were from Gilford, New Hampshire, where they owned a house on Lake Winnipesaukee.

"Last year we sailed from Barcelona to Cartegena. The year before that was the Toulon to Barcelona leg. We've been working our way along the northern Mediterranean."

It didn't take much encouragement to get them to join us for a late dinner. Afterward we sat in the salon and learned a bit more about them.

"We should really be back in New Hampshire this time of year. These two weeks are among the busiest of the year for our restaurant," Joan told us.

"Yeah," Dwayne said, "but we leave it in the capable hands of our son and his wife. Along with our partner Troy, they really run the place these days."

"What type of restaurant is it?" I asked, wondering if it was a fast-food type place or something fancy.

Joan took a sip of her tea, and replied, "It's a full-service family restaurant. We also have a few rooms upstairs that we rent out, sort of an inn."

Maeve smiled as she offered to refill Joan's cup. "It sounds like a bed-and-breakfast."

Joan held her cup out to let Maeve top it off and shook her head.

"Not really; we don't actually serve breakfast." She laughed. "But you can sleep in late and come down for lunch."

While the ladies talked about the restaurant, Dwayne and I talked about sailing.

"Lake Winnipesaukee is a good-sized body of water, isn't it?" I asked Dwayne.

He nodded thoughtfully. "It's twenty miles from

Moultonborough to Alton Bay and five miles or more wide, depending on how you measure."

"How long is the sailing season?" I asked, wondering what it would be like to sail that lake. I imagined it would be a lot like the time Hans and I visited his grandmother and went sailing on Lake Geneva.

"Ice out usually occurs about the third week of April," Dwayne explained, "but it's usually another couple of weeks before I put the boat back in the water."

He noticed the puzzled look on my face when he said ice out.

"Ice out is declared when there is enough open water for the Mount Washington to make all its ports."

I'd heard of the Motor Vessel Mount Washington. It made regular rounds of the lake during the late spring, summer, and early fall. My mother, who was from southwestern New Hampshire, had visited Lake Winnipesaukee and cruised aboard the M/V Mount Washington.

The vessel was named for the real Mount Washington, the highest mountain in New England, and the location of the highest wind speed ever recorded. When I was a kid we'd visited it once or twice, but I hadn't been in a long time.

"You and Maeve should come up and visit some time," Dwayne suggested. "I'll take you out sailing on the lake. You'll love it."

As it was getting late, he suggested this as they were preparing to row back to their boat.

"We will definitely plan on it," I promised as I helped Joan down into their dinghy.

We didn't see them the next morning as they rose with the sun and headed west. We did hear them, though, as they weighed anchor and hoisted their sails.

"They were a nice couple," Maeve noted. "I hope we'll still be traveling the world to go sailing when we're that age."

"As long as we can, we will," I assured her.

We spent a couple of days seeing the sites around Almunecar before continuing our voyage. We spent another month sailing east along the Spanish coast, finally arriving in Valencia. There we turned in our trusty vessel and rested for a few days before boarding the first of the several flights it would take to get us home.

Five

We arrived in Raleigh and spent another night in the Hilton before loading up on the Cessna and flying back to Wilmington. Since we had a couple of weeks before Maeve started teaching at Laney and I started classes at UNCW, we decided to spend them at River Dream.

Before we could do that, though, we had to visit her folks and my folks and tell them all about our trip. Malori was especially interested in hearing all about our adventures. After a lasagna dinner at Mom and Dad's, she bombarded us with questions.

"Did you have to speak Spanish the whole time?" she wanted to know.

"I don't know that we had to," Maeve told her, "but since both of us are pretty good at it, we usually did."

"After a day ashore doing the tourist thing," I added, "we'd catch ourselves talking in Spanish to each other on the boat without thinking about it."

Malori laughed. "That sounds kind of cool. If you go to France next time, are you going to learn French first?"

"Je parle francais, un peur," I replied. "I already know a

little from high school. With a few lessons, I think we could manage."

Malori was most interested in the horseback riding.

"You rode western-style American saddles in the middle of Spain?" she asked incredulously.

"The whole place was styled after a South Dakota dude ranch," Maeve told her.

As the discussion became more about horses, I tuned out. When Maeve and Malori started talking horses, they entered a zone all their own. The two of them, it turned out, had found common ground.

Malori's interest in riding had blossomed while I was away in the Navy. Most days she'd much rather ride than go sailing, which was close to blasphemy in my book.

My ears perked up when I heard Malori say, "Why don't you come riding with me next weekend?"

Maeve looked at me.

I shrugged and said, "Sure. It'll mean staying in town, but we've got nothing planned that I know of."

Maeve smiled at Malori. "Then I'd love to."

"Great," Malori said. "You can ride Darling."

Darling, a chestnut brown Morgan mare with such a gentle disposition the owner of the stable often borrowed her to give younger kids their first ride, was the older of Malori's two horses. She'd been Malori's first horse.

"And you'll get to meet Debonaire, my quarter horse," Malori continued. "He's a gelding, but he's still got lots of spirit."

The next evening found us in Whiteville dining with the Daltons. Much to our surprise, our trip wasn't the big news of the night.

After dinner, when we were all seated in the living room, Cynthia requested the floor.

"I know this will come as a shock, since you didn't know I was seeing anyone, but I'm getting married."

We all looked at her in stunned silence for a moment. Finally Maeve found her voice.

"Wow, that's a surprise; congratulations, Cynthia. Who's the lucky guy?"

"Yes, dear," Phyllis managed to say. "Who is this fellow you've been keeping a secret from us all?"

Ted stood up, his face twisted into a puzzled frown, and sat down again.

Cynthia's gaze traveled over each of us before she replied. "His name is Andrew Crispman. He's a major in the Army. I met him last month when he transferred in. It was love at first sight."

Ted's mouth was set firmly as he nodded while Cynthia talked.

"When will we get to meet this major?" he asked tersely when Cynthia paused.

His tone caused Cynthia to react as though he'd struck her. Maeve and Phyllis both seemed surprised by the harshness in his voice. I felt it best if I kept a low profile.

"Well, I'm sorry," Ted continued. "We didn't even know she was seeing anyone. She's known the guy barely a month, and already she's talking about getting married."

"Maeve and Michael hardly knew each other longer than that when they got married," Cynthia retorted.

Her hand flew to her mouth as if trying to stop the words that already escaped. She turned to Maeve to apologize, but she was too late.

"If you'll recall, big sister, Michael and I had known each other for years before the time was right for us to get together. It was hardly a whirlwind romance."

It hurt me to see the tears forming in Maeve's eyes. I

reached out and put my arm around her. The look on Cynthia's face could only be described as panic.

"I didn't mean it, Maeve. I'm so sorry."

She stepped toward Maeve, but Maeve turned her head into my shoulder to hide her tears.

At last Phyllis spoke. "I think maybe we all need to calm down here. Cynthia has presented us with what I think is happy news. Ted, I'm ashamed of you, reacting that way. After all, you asked me to get married little more than a month after we met."

She said this last with a coy smile and eyes that dared him to contradict her.

Ted drew a deep breath and slowly let it out, his lips pressed into a thin line. His head swiveled as his eyes bore first into his wife, and then into Cynthia. It must have been the heartbroken look on Cynthia's face that penetrated his anger and made him realize what his reaction was doing to her.

"I'm sorry that I'm not overjoyed by your news, sweetheart. It comes a quite a shock."

He turned to Phyllis, and said, "We haven't even met this guy. She hardly even knows this guy. How can you blame me for reacting like an overprotective father when she springs something like this on us out of the blue?"

Cynthia, straining to keep her voice steady, said, "Daddy, when you meet him, I just know you'll like him. Andrew is a very special man and I really do love him. Daddy, you know me. I wouldn't even think of marrying him if I wasn't absolutely sure."

Clasping his hands under his chin, Ted looked into Cynthia's eyes and saw the tears there, threatening to fall.

"You've never given me a reason to doubt your judgment before, Cynthia. I suppose I should at least meet your young man before I decide he's not good enough for my daughter." His lips turned up in a weak smile. "Okay?"

Cynthia nodded her head and blinked back her tears. "Okay, Dad. Yeah, that'll be okay."

Turning away from her father, Cynthia asked Maeve, "How about us? Are we okay?"

Maeve sniffed, wiped away a tear, and then smiled a genuine smile. "Yeah, we're okay."

Phyllis heaved a big sigh of relief. A family disaster had been averted.

Cynthia then went on to explain, "Andrew was going to come tonight to meet everyone, but duty called and he had to work. I wanted it to be a surprise. That was foolish, I guess."

Feeling it might be safe, I spoke up. "It worked. Everyone was sure surprised."

Cynthia stuck her tongue out at me, and we all laughed.

Phyllis announced it was time for dessert. She'd baked a German chocolate cake, which was quite rich and tasty. Following dessert, Maeve and I entertained them with stories of our voyage. It was well after midnight when we finally returned to our house on Wrightsville Beach.

Six

Though I'd learned horseback riding as a kid, I never fell in love with the sport the way Malori and, as I was coming to discover, Maeve did. Since I had no interest in hanging around the stables while the two of them were horsing around, I convinced my father that we should take his new boat out fishing. Dad explained why he'd bought the boat he did as he showed me around his Grady-White 255 Sailfish with its twin 140-horsepower Johnson motors.

"When I decided it was time for a new boat, I looked at what there was out there and remembered what you told me about Derrick's dad's boat. When I saw the Sailfish, I knew it was just what I was looking for."

We cast off and headed offshore. A couple of hours cruising later and we were at the wreck of the *Cassimir*, a 400-foot tanker built just after World War I. The *Cassimir* sank in a collision with the SS *Lara* in 1942 while carrying molasses from Cuba to Baltimore. The wreck was a popular fishing and diving site. My father and I had fished there often when I was a kid.

We spent the day trying different spots around the

wreck. The fish were pretty lazy, and we didn't catch many. Those we did we released anyway. Giving the fish a break at mid-day, we enjoyed the picnic lunch my mom packed for us. Around mid-afternoon we decided to head back, arriving just in time for dinner.

Maeve was waiting for us on the dock as we pulled up. Actually, she and Malori were sitting in the cockpit of *Hey 19*, my first sailboat. She was a nineteen-foot West-White Potter.

"Ahoy, *Hey 19*," I called out as we got close.

Maeve smiled, waved, and called back, "How was the fishing?"

She jumped quickly to the dock, followed by Malori, to handle the lines as my father pulled the Sailfish alongside.

Tossing Maeve the bowline, I told her, "So-so. We got a few bites but let them go."

Maeve's lips turned down in an exaggerated pout. "No fish for supper, then."

I laughed at her expression. "No, I'm afraid not."

"Who's a frayed knot?" Malori joked. "Where are all the fish?"

Dad handed me the poles and said, "We left them in the ocean so they would stay fresh."

Malori gave him an "awe, Dad," and ran off to tell Mom we were back.

Putting my arm around Maeve I asked, "How long have you guys been back from horsing?"

She pursed her lips. "Is that a real verb?"

I shrugged. She was the English teacher; she ought to know.

"We got back about an hour ago. After riding, I took Malori to lunch at Dupree's, and then we did some shopping. Darling is a great horse. How come you never told me Malori was so into riding?"

I shrugged again. "I guess it never came up. Haven't you noticed all the horse stuff in her room?"

It was Maeve's turn to shrug. "No big deal. I know now. We had a great time riding together."

My father lifted his tackle box onto the dock. That was not as easy as it sounded. His offshore fishing tackle box looked like a decent-sized mechanic's toolbox. Then he reached back and lifted the now empty cooler out of the boat.

I handed Maeve the poles. "If you'll carry these up to the house, I'll grab the tackle box."

That left my father with only the cooler to worry about. The cooler was empty so it would be easy for him.

Mom and Malori came down to see what was taking the rest of us so long. By then I was playing the hose over the rods and reels to clean as much salt water off them as possible. Dad had put his tackle box away in his equipment room. Maeve was sitting on the cooler telling me all about her day at the stable with Malori.

"First we exercised them in the paddock so they could stretch out and warm up some. Then we tacked up and walked them around the paddock until Darling got used to me being in the saddle."

Maeve was smiling as she talked about it. "She didn't seem to mind at all that it was me and not Malori. Once I felt comfortable enough, we took them out on the trail around the stables."

I knew the trail they meant. It meandered through the woods and fields around the horse farm for about two miles.

"After the ride we brushed them down and turned them out to the pasture to graze. It was a great morning."

I'd been listening while I made sure to do a good job of cleaning the fishing gear. Deciding I'd done a thorough job, I turned off the water.

"So, where did you go shopping after you were done horsing around?"

From the deck Malori answered for her. "We went shopping for boots, that's what. Maeve had to ride in sneakers because she doesn't have any riding boots. We fixed that."

Rewinding the hose on its reel, I asked Maeve, "You bought riding boots? Are you planning to do a lot of riding then?"

Again, Malori answered for her. "I told her anytime she wanted to take me to the stables, we can go riding."

Maeve added, "And I did tell her that anytime we were in town, and I had the time, we would go."

My father came out of his equipment room, having put everything away just so.

"Why don't we get washed up and find out what's for dinner?"

Malori and Maeve traded a conspiratorial look.

My mother said from the deck, "We won't know what's for dinner until we find out what the King Neptune has on special."

My father looked up and asked, "When did we decide to go to the King Neptune?"

My mother replied, "We ladies decided we would like seafood and were fairly certain you two would not bring back any."

She turned away with a smug look and went inside. Maeve and Malori giggled at us before running up the stairs. My father and I traded defeated looks and went in to wash up.

Flounder, my mom's favorite, was the special at the King Neptune that night. My father ordered the flounder and shrimp combination. Malori joined our mother in having the flounder in a smaller portion. Maeve and I both chose the surf and turf. I always loved the taste of shrimp and sirloin together. We said good-bye in the parking lot after dinner, and Maeve and I went to our house for the night. The next morning we were up early to fly home to River Dream.

Seven

We'd been home at River Dream for a few days when the subject of horses came up. Two days spent cleaning house and grocery shopping had left me longing to get on the water. We rigged Riverscape after lunch and sailed a big triangle across the river toward Cherry Branch, downriver to Great Neck Point, and then home.

The final leg was actually more of a zig-zag as we were beating to weather against a northwest wind. After supper we sat in the swing in the screened room sipping iced tea and enjoying the breeze.

"Sweetheart," Maeve began in the voice she used when about to suggest something she figured I probably wouldn't want to do. "Sweetheart, don't you think we could put up a little stable in that field behind the house? Maybe fence off a pasture for a horse?"

I'd known this was coming. Trying to postpone the inevitable, I pointed out, "Babe, we don't have a horse."

Maeve rolled her eyes and looked at me over the top of her Foster-Grants. "I know we don't have a horse. I think it would be nice to get one. Having my own horse was a dream of mine when I was a girl."

"You've never talked about it before," I said. "What brought this on all of a sudden?"

Maeve turned to face me on the swing. "I started thinking about it again when we were on that overnight ride in Spain. Then the other day when I went riding with Malori the idea just grew on me. These last couple of days I've been trying to decide if it's something I really want to get involved in again. Bad news, sweetheart, I do."

"That's what I was afraid of," I said, resigning myself to the fact that we were going to be getting a horse; however, there were some things I wanted to make sure she had considered.

"Maeve, even if we do build a stable here, what about when we're back at Wrightsville Beach? Where would we keep the horse while we're gone? Who would take care of it?"

She was ready with an answer. "We could stable it here in Pamlico. They would take care of it and I would ride it on weekends when we come home."

Looking out toward the dock, I observed, "It won't fit on the boat."

Maeve chuckled, knowing that was my way of saying yes. "No, I don't imagine it will. We wouldn't give up sailing. It would just be something else we could do."

Shaking my head slowly, I was completely honest with her. "It would have to be something you would do. I have no interest in riding horses. That trail ride in Spain convinced me of that."

As much as I'd enjoyed our time at the ranch, it hadn't done my bionic hip a lot of good. After that ride I decided I'd take sail canvas over saddle leather every time.

Maeve had known spending that much time on a horse had been something of an endurance test for me, though I hadn't said anything. I hated being reminded that there were some things I just couldn't do as well as I could before getting wounded.

"All right. Then it'll be something I do. I'll ride and you can watch me," she said.

"I guess we can think about it," I conceded.

Of course by that I meant that we would get her a horse and she knew it. I could tell by the satisfied smile on her face. After spending a month and a half living on a boat, I guess I could understand why Maeve might want to take up a hobby that would keep her on dry land once in a while.

Maeve started researching what kind of horse would be best for her. We spent a good bit of our time over the days remaining before we had to go back to school - Maeve as a rookie English teacher at Laney, me as a sophomore at UNCW - traveling eastern North Carolina looking at horses. Maeve decided on either a Morgan Horse or a Quarter Horse.

As luck would have it, right in Pamlico County, she found a four-year-old that was half of each, a jet black mare named Raven. Maeve fell in love with Raven the first time she saw her.

"I know she's my horse. I knew it as soon as I looked at her."

Raven seemed to respond to Maeve as well. She had her horse.

Raven was being kept at R&R Stables. The owners of R&R, Ray and Rita Gallagher, were happy to let us keep Raven there and look after her for us. Rita and Maeve were destined to become good friends.

We also built a stall and paddock behind the house at River Dream so that Maeve could bring Raven home on those occasions when we could be there more than a few days at a time.

Seeing an opportunity for myself in this, I told Maeve, "You realize that in order to carry Raven back and forth we'll need a horse trailer."

Maeve recognized that glint in my eye. "I suppose we will," she agreed.

Pressing the matter, I continued, "And I don't think the old Jeep will be able to pull any reasonably sized trailer."

Maeve smiled. "Are you trying to say you want to buy a new truck?"

Putting on my best innocent face, I replied, "Only because I think you'll need one to pull your horse trailer."

Maeve laughed out loud at that. "Michael Justin Lanier, you know perfectly well that you can afford to go out and buy any truck you want anytime you want."

She was right about that.

"What you say it true," I acknowledged. "However, I feel better spending the money for a good reason than just because I have it to spend."

The next day found us in New Bern at the Jeep dealership looking over what they had that might do the job. A blue Jeep Laredo four-wheel-drive pickup with a 360 V-8 seemed to be just the vehicle for the job, so it became ours. The dealership took the old CJ in trade more out of pity for it than anything else.

Once we had a truck with which to tow, it was time to find a horse trailer to tow. I was thinking we would get a simple, straightforward horse trailer that could carry a couple of horses. Maeve had other ideas.

She'd seen the Gallaghers' trailer, the one they used for going to rodeos and horse shows. It had room for three horses, a small tack room, and a tiny bunk room. Maeve's enthusiasm for that large a trailer dimmed somewhat when I reminded her that she'd be the one towing it and backing it.

"How often do you think you'll be going off overnight with Raven?" I asked Maeve as we were sitting in the den at home looking over the brochures we'd picked up.

"I don't know," she replied absently, comparing the trailers on the covers of two of the brochures. "It could be a lot or a little. Maybe Malori would like to come up and go with me to some things."

I knew she was probably right about that. Eventually, we decided on a two-horse trailer with a changing room that was just big enough to put down a couple of sleeping bags.

Eight

It seemed like we'd barely gotten the horse situation figured out when it was time to go back to school. Maeve was teaching English Composition One and Two, three classes of freshmen and two of sophomores. I was beginning my sophomore year of college. Maeve's first workday preceded my first day of class by two days.

"What are you going to be doing for two days while I'm hard at work?" Maeve asked me the last night before she started her teaching career. She was looking over all the things she planned to take with her to school the next day.

Watching her pack and re-pack everything in her tote bags and boxes, I couldn't help but chuckle. "Maybe we should've brought the horse trailer down for you to pack it all in. It might have been big enough."

"Very funny," Maeve retorted. "I want to make sure I'm prepared."

Smiling at her defensiveness, I said, "You should certainly be prepared for anything."

Judging from the dark look Maeve gave me, I don't think she was amused. I finally realized she was more nervous than she'd let on.

"Babe, you're gonna do fine. You'll be a great teacher, and the kids will love you."

Maeve had shown me the glowing recommendation Miss Preston, her student teaching coach, wrote when Maeve applied for the position at Laney.

"Miss Preston doesn't hand out praise lightly, and she thinks you've got what it takes." I smiled, remembering my days in Miss Preston's class. "I can't believe she's still teaching."

Maeve looked at me, and I was surprised to see tears in her eyes. "Do you really think I'll do okay?"

I got up from my desk and pulled her to me. "You will be the best thing that ever happened to those kids," I promised her as I took her in a bear hug.

She clung to me tightly for a moment, and then relaxed. "Thanks," she said. "I needed that."

Her moment of crisis passed, and the confident Maeve returned.

"You still haven't answered my question," she reminded me.

"What question was that?" I replied innocently, sitting back down at my desk.

Maeve lowered her head and looked at me with raised eyebrows.

"Oh, that question," I snickered. "Tomorrow I'll go by the campus bookstore to get my textbooks and other assorted stuff for classes. The next day I figured I would go fishing."

Her expression left no doubt she didn't like that idea.

"Or I could come to school with you and help you get your room ready."

Her smile left no doubt she thought that was the better plan.

Why seeing Derrick in the college book store the next morning surprised me, I don't know. He'd called a few days before to let me know he was home from Parris Island, having survived Marine Corps basic training. We'd planned on meeting for lunch at the Seahawks' Nest later that same day.

Maybe it wasn't seeing him that surprised me. Rather, it was seeing the change in him. Derrick was always fit and trim from his martial arts training, but now his muscles bulged under the red Marine Corps t-shirt he was wearing. And this new Derrick had no hair to speak of. He'd always worn it short. Now there was nothing but stubble.

Derrick noticed me staring at his nearly bald scalp. "It'll grow back," he said as he reached up to rub his head. "But not much. Gotta keep it short now."

"You look good," I said, reaching out to shake his hand. "Marine training must agree with you."

"I'm not so sure it agreed with me, but it didn't kill me," Derrick said, with a dry chuckle. "It wasn't as bad as I thought it would be, but it was no day at the beach."

We finished up our business at the book store and headed to the Nest where we swapped training stories over an early lunch.

As we finished up our lunch, I invited Derrick to the house for dinner.

"I'm sure Maeve would love to see you," I said. Actually, inviting Derrick over had been her idea.

"Ah, man," Derrick said, shaking his head sadly. "That sounds good, but I already have plans. Do you remember Vanessa?"

"Isn't she the girl whose dad owns Del Mar out in Nags Head?"

"That's her. She's in town visiting her cousin from Durham who's going to school here. Tomorrow she heads back to State for the fall semester. We're all going out tonight."

"Sounds cool," I said. "Another time then."

"You know it," Derrick said, clapping me on the back. "I'll see ya, Mike."

He jogged off toward his car. I walked back to mine, admiring how nice the GTO still looked for a twenty-year-old car.

I'd been home about an hour, organizing my materials and schedules for the classes that'd be starting in a couple days, when Maeve arrived fresh from her teacher work day. She had her arms full of books and binders.

"How was your first work day?" I asked as I took a stack of books from her.

Her chest heaved with a big sigh, but a smile curled her lips. "It was busy, busy, busy," she said. "There's so much that has to be done before Open House. And all us Initially Licensed Teachers have an ILT meeting tomorrow at Central Office all day. I don't know when I'm going to get all this done."

I set her books down at *her* end of the table in our office-slash-study. My stuff was still spread out all over the other end.

Picking up and looking at what must have been a grammar book, I asked, "How soon is Open House?"

She dropped the rest of her burden on the table and pushed back a few locks of strawberry blond hair that had fallen in her eyes. "It's the day after tomorrow."

"And you have to spend all day tomorrow in a meeting?" I asked, eyes wide. "That sure doesn't leave you much time to get ready."

Maeve shook her head, causing those errant locks of hair to fall into her eyes again.

"No, it doesn't. That's why I brought all this home. Looks like I'm in for a late night."

"I guess it's a good thing I've already taken care of supper," I told her. "So you get organized while I set the table."

Maeve's eyes grew wide in surprise. "You cooked?"

A sheepish grin crossed my face. "Uh, to be honest, no, I didn't. Actually, I ordered calzones from Dupree's. They should be here any minute."

"I should have known," Maeve said, shaking her head, but she was smiling.

Over supper, Maeve looked at me, pointing her knife and fork at the half a calzone left on her plate. "Why did you order two? We never finish them."

"Leftovers," I replied. "Now we don't have to worry about what to have tomorrow night."

Maeve rolled her eyes and took a final bite. After washing it down with the last of her iced tea, she looked up and said, "Did I tell you the first football game was this Friday?"

"Do you want to go?" I asked. "We can leave for River Dream first thing Saturday morning."

"Nah, it's an away game. The next week is at home; we'll go to that one."

"All right," I said. "We'll plan on that then."

I got up and went to the cabinet to find containers for our leftovers.

"Did I mention that I saw Derrick at the book store this morning?"

Maeve took the containers from me. "I knew you were supposed to have lunch with him today. It makes sense that he was at the book store, too. How's he doing?"

"He looked good. Basic training didn't hurt him any."

Maeve laughed. "I didn't think it would. Did you tell him I'm still mad at him about missing our wedding?"

"I told him that's why I couldn't invite him to supper tonight," I said, trying hard to keep a straight face.

Maeve slammed the refrigerator door and turned to me. "Michael J. Lanier, you did not."

I turned to the sink so she couldn't see the grin on my face. "Well, of course I did."

She moved up behind me and I felt a sudden pain as she pinched my neck. "You better be kidding, mister."

Spinning around, I grabbed her in a bear hug. "Of course I'm kidding."

I bent forward and kissed the frown off her lips.

"I asked him to come for dinner, but he had plans. Vanessa's in town visiting her cousin, and they were going out tonight."

Maeve pressed her hands against my chest and looked up at me, her heather blue eyes sparkling with mischief. "Well, okay then. I suppose you can have dessert."

Nine

The rest of the week went by in a blur as Maeve and I got busy with our new academic years. Before we knew it, Friday afternoon arrived.

We'd barely gotten the Cessna tied down before Maeve was ready to head to the stable to see Raven.

"Don't you think we should stop by the house first?" I inquired reasonably.

Maeve gave me a glare. "I'll drop you off if you want; I'm going to see my horse."

I didn't feel like going to the stable, so I let her drop me off. Thus, a routine was born. Saturdays became Maeve's riding days.

During football season, if Laney had a home game, we would go to the game and wait to fly home Saturday morning. Otherwise, we'd fly up on Friday evening. Early Saturday, Maeve would rise, cook us breakfast, and head to the stables for her lessons. The joy she took in learning to ride and getting to know Raven made me happy for her.

We still sailed. One weekend a month Raven would have to settle for a Friday night visit so that Maeve and I could spend the weekend on the water. If the wind and the weather were right, we would sail to Ocracoke and spend the night. Less favorable conditions might see us sail and motor to Morehead City for dinner at the Sanitary Fish Market. Other times we might sail upriver to New Bern, tie up at Union Point Park and walk to dinner at one of the restaurants downtown. Eventually the shorter days and colder weather limited our sailing to the waters close to home.

The shorter days and longer nights also meant the semester was coming to an end. Maeve had a good first semester and was, for the most part, happy being a teacher. My semester went well, too. Only taking four classes meant less homework and less stress. Maeve was against my doing that at first, until I reminded her I really didn't need to hurry and finish my degree.

Semester's end also meant the arrival of the holiday season. With Christmas coming up, Maeve told me Mr. McHale had polled the faculty about where they would like to have the staff luncheon.

"Mr. McHale told us at the staff meeting that some kind soul had offered to pick up the check so we could eat out at a nice place instead of having a pot luck buffet in the cafeteria," Maeve said. "You wouldn't know anything about that, would you, Michael?"

I gave her my best *aw shucks* grin. "Well, I might have mentioned something to Mr. McHale about y'all having a nice party off campus. Where'd you decide to go?"

"The overwhelming favorite was Primavera's, the new Italian restaurant that opened up on Market Street last spring."

"Primavera's, huh? I don't know about an Italian restaurant that doesn't serve pizza," I said. "What is it Mr. DeLuca says, 'Primavera's serves fine Italian cuisine which, in my opinion, does not include pizza.' His prices certainly reflect how fine he thinks his Italian cuisine is."

Maeve wrinkled her brow. "Having second thoughts about your offer?"

I shook my head. "No, a deal's a deal. And when we ate there, the food was pretty good."

"Yeah," Maeve said. "I remember you weren't very impressed. Didn't you say you'd rather have a pizza at Dupree's?"

I rolled my eyes and laughed. "Babe, I'd rather have Dupree's pizza than just about anything else."

Her eyes narrowed, and I added, "Except your cooking, of course. Still, the staff voted for Primavera's, so Primavera's it'll be."

According to the story Maeve related to me later, on the last teacher work day before Christmas, the staff left campus on an activity bus and made their way to Primavera's. Upon arriving, they were welcomed by the maitre d' who informed Mr. McHale that the bus would have to park behind the building as it was an eyesore. Somewhat taken aback, Mr. McHale had the driver move the bus once all the teachers had gotten off.

That taken care of, they approached the front door only to be told that they would have to wait outside until the room was ready for them. As it was twelve-thirty, the time they were supposed to be there, this did not sit well with Mr. McHale. The maitre d' did not seem too concerned, so Mr. McHale asked to speak to the manager or to Mr. DeLuca. The maitre d' sniffed imperiously and told them that perhaps the room was ready and they should follow him.

Primavera's had an ample banquet room, but it didn't appear much effort had gone into setting it up for their luncheon. After moving some of the chairs and tables themselves, the staff sat down and waited for their waiters and waitresses to arrive and begin taking orders. Twenty minutes later, they were still waiting. Mr. McHale went and found the maitre d' and inquired politely if they might expect service soon.

"We will get to you teachers when we get to you," the maitre d' informed Mr. McHale before sticking his nose in the air and turning his back on the principal.

Mr. McHale again asked to speak to Mr. DeLuca, at which point the maitre d' walked away from him and directed one of the waitresses who had been standing by the wait station to go see what those teachers wanted to drink. Mr. McHale returned to the banquet room.

I later learned from talking to Mr. DeLuca that, unbeknownst to Mr. McHale, the maitre d' went to Mr. DeLuca's office and told him those teachers were in the banquet room and demanding to be served.

Mr. DeLuca'd made a sour face. "Who do they think they are? How is it teachers are even being paid enough to dine in my restaurant? I will let them know that they should be grateful for the privilege and should mind their manners."

I pieced together what happened next from several different versions of the story I heard after the fact.

The waitress had just finished taking the drink orders when Mr. DeLuca stormed in.

"I don't know who you people think you are, but you do not come into my restaurant making demands of my staff. You are only teachers, after all. It is a crime that you are even paid enough to think about being able to dine here at my establishment. Now, you sit there and mind your manners and be glad I have decided to let you stay."

Maeve and the rest of the staff sat there dumbfounded. Never had they imagined anyone would ever speak to them that way, especially not a business owner who they thought would appreciate their trade. Mr. McHale certainly wasn't going to sit idly by while his staff was abused so.

"Now see here, DeLuca, we'll save you the trouble of deciding to let us stay. We're leaving."

Mr. DeLuca shook his head slowly, a look of imperious condescension on his face. "Oh, I think not. We have already begun preparing your meals. You will not leave until you have paid for each and every one."

Ten

At that opportune moment, I walked in, in the company of two detectives from the Wilmington Police Department whose wives taught with Maeve at the high school. The senior detective, Jason Lewis, whose brother had played with me on the soccer team, realized there was some kind of situation brewing.

"Is there some kind of a problem here?" Jason asked Mr. DeLuca.

Mr. DeLuca turned his arrogant gaze on Jason. "And just who are you?" he sneered.

"Detective Sergeant Jason Lewis, Wilmington PD," responded Jason in a courteous and professional way.

"Very well, detective, I want these…teachers…arrested." Mr. DeLuca said teachers as if it left a bad taste in his mouth.

Jason kept a straight face only through an enormous effort. He carefully avoided making eye contact with his wife. "Just what have they done, Mr. DeLuca?"

Mr. DeLuca put his hands on his hips and sputtered, "They are trying to leave without paying for their meals."

D W Davis

"What meals? Have you folks had any meals?" Jason asked the teachers. Looking around the banquet room, he noted, "There are no plates on the tables."

Mr. DeLuca practically snorted, "Of course there are no plates on the tables. They haven't been served yet."

His tone made it plain he thought Jason should have figured this out on his own.

Mr. McHale, knowing exactly who Jason, Paul, and I were, stepped forward. "As a matter of fact, detective, we haven't even ordered yet."

Mr. DeLuca's eyes flashed. "You just shut your mouth," he commanded Mr. McHale.

Mr. DeLuca turned on Jason, "Call in a paddy wagon or whatever you have to do, detective, but I demand you arrest all of them."

Jason took a deep breath to compose himself before saying, "Mr. DeLuca, you want me to arrest a room full of teachers because they have not paid for food you haven't even prepared, for meals they haven't even ordered? Is that correct?"

"Yes!" Mr. DeLuca said emphatically, apparently glad the cop finally understood the situation.

Jason looked around the room, finally catching his wife's eye. She was trying to hide a smile. We all wondered if Mr. DeLuca had any idea at all of how ridiculous he sounded. I looked at Maeve, but she wouldn't look my way. Later she said that she was afraid if she looked at me she would start laughing and wouldn't be able to stop.

Mr. McHale wasn't laughing. I thought he was going to explode, and realized I needed to do something.

"Sgt. Lewis, I think I should take Mr. McHale here outside and get his side of the story."

Jason looked at me in confusion at first. After all, I

wasn't a cop. But he went along.

"Good idea, Lanier. Detective Patrick and I will stay here and keep an eye on the rest of these suspects."

Jason barely managed to keep a straight face as he said this. Mr. DeLuca stood there fuming. The teachers were talking quietly among themselves. They all knew who Jason, Paul Patrick, and I were, especially that those two were cops.

Mr. McHale wasn't sure what to think, but he followed me outside. "Michael, when did you join the Police Department?"

I looked back toward the banquet room to be sure we were out of earshot. "About thirty seconds ago, sir. I think I've been deputized by silent consent. Mr. DeLuca doesn't know that. Come on, let's you and I go use the payphone. I assume you won't be staying here for lunch."

Mr. McHale made a derisive noise deep in his throat. "You assume correctly, young man. Who are you going to call?"

There was only one person I could think of who could handle a group like that on short notice, Alfred Dupree.

"I am going to call an old friend of mine. Your staff wanted Italian. I hope they'll settle for pizza."

I called Alfred and asked him if, as a personal favor to me, he could make up enough pizza to feed the staff at Laney High and do so in the next hour. All he asked was if they were coming there or if I needed them delivered.

"I can't imagine you've got room for all of them," I said.

"Nonsense, Michael. The lunch crowd has started thinning out. You bring them over, and I'll have a place for them," Alfred assured me.

"Thank you so much for this, Alfred. I really owe you one."

"Don't be silly, Michael. It's the least I can do for such a good friend as you."

Mr. McHale seemed relieved to hear the situation had been taken care of, at least that part of the situation.

My next call was to my father. "Dad, I need to know the details of Mr. DeLuca's lease on the Primavera's building."

"What in the world for, son?" my father asked, surprise evident in his voice.

If I was going to get the teachers out of there before the situation became any more ridiculous, I couldn't take the time to go into detail. "I promise I'll explain later. I just need to know if there's anything in the terms that would allow me to evict him."

Astonished, my father said, "You want to evict him? What's going on?"

"I promise, Dad, I'll explain later. Right now I just need to know if there is a clause or something that will allow me to threaten him with eviction."

My father, trusting that I knew what I was doing, asked me, "Has he damaged the building, done something illegal, impaired his ability to do business in some way that would keep him from being able to pay the rent? I'm not sure of the exact terms of his lease, but those are fairly standard things."

Nodding to myself, I replied, "Oh, you could say he has impaired his ability to do business. Once word gets out of how he treated the Laney teachers today, he may never get another customer through the door. Thanks, Dad, I have to go."

Mr. McHale was eying me skeptically as I hung up the phone. "Michael, I know you have connections, but how are you going to evict DeLuca?" Disdain dripped from his voice as he said the restaurateur's name.

I gave him a brief explanation. "It's easy, Mr. McHale. I own the building, and Mr. DeLuca just severely impacted his ability to meet the rent in a very negative way."

"Oh." That was all Mr. McHale said, but a big smile spread across his face.

I told him that as soon as he could get the staff back on the bus he should take them to Dupree's Pizza. Alfred would be expecting them. Then it was time for me to have a little fun.

As Mr. McHale and I returned to the banquet room, we heard Jason trying to explain to an irate Mr. DeLuca why he couldn't arrest the teachers.

"Mr. DeLuca, sir, please understand that you have no cause to arrest anyone here. It isn't a crime to change your mind about eating at a restaurant."

Before Mr. DeLuca could respond, I intervened.

"DeLuca," I said, harshly and with deliberate disrespect, "you have more important things to worry about right now than this fine group of educators. You need to start trying to find another location for your restaurant."

Eleven

Mr. DeLuca turned toward me so fast he almost lost his balance.

"What do you mean? Who do you think you are? You're just a lousy cop."

I felt a chilling smile cross my face. "That was probably a poor choice of words, DeLuca. I am not a police officer, nor did I ever claim to be. I merely offered to take Mr. McHale to the other room as I needed to talk to him. If I were a cop, however, I could probably make a good case against you for unlawful detention. Several good cases in fact, as many cases as there are teachers in this room."

I turned to Jason and asked him, "Am I right about that, Sergeant Lewis?"

"I'm sure the District Attorney would want to at least look into the allegations, should any of these fine educators choose to press the issue," Jason said with a barely suppressed grin.

Confusion showed on Mr. DeLuca's face. "What, what, wait a minute here! Who are you then, if you're not a cop?"

At that point I knew I had him. "That, DeLuca, I think

we should discuss in private."

Something in my tone must have gotten through that thick skull of his. "Very well, we will go to my office."

There were some things I wanted made clear first. "And the teachers, they are free to go," I asked, "without any more threats or accusations?"

Mr. DeLuca did not look as though he liked that idea. "Yes, alright, get them out of here. I won't press charges."

Jason looked at me with a puzzled expression, but Mr. McHale took him aside and whispered something to him. Jason looked up and gave me a nod. Paul began ushering the staff out the door. Maeve started to come over to me, but I waved her off. I mouthed to her that I would tell her later. She shrugged and followed the rest of the staff out the door.

At least there had been no other customers in the restaurant. Primavera's usually only opened at lunch time for special parties - parties like a teacher's luncheon.

Mr. DeLuca and I went to his office.

"Okay, so who are you that McHale and those lousy cops let you take charge of things that way?" he asked, trying to regain some of his bluster.

I walked past him, sat down in his chair, and folded my hands on his desk. Looking up at him as if he was a misbehaving child, I said, "He is Mr. McHale to you, and those two cops are fine law enforcement officers. You, on the other hand, run a gussied-up, tomato-paste diner and have a way too overinflated opinion of yourself and your out-of-a-can culinary concoctions."

Mr. DeLuca turned scarlet and raged, "How dare you, you young punk?"

In a calm, icy, voice I replied, "I dare, DeLuca, because I can. You see, your lease is with Coastal Carolina Realty Trust. My name is Michael Lanier. I own Coastal Carolina

Realty Trust."

For the first time, Mr. DeLuca had no quick come-back.
A worried look flitted across his face.

"I also own the Coastal Carolina Small Business Fund, the
company that loaned you the money to get this place up and
running. That loan is callable at any time, DeLuca. I'm calling
it."

Mr. DeLuca slumped into one of the uncomfortable
chairs he no doubt made his employees sit in when they came
into his office. "Impossible, I cannot pay."

With a shark's grin and cold hard eyes, I informed him,
"Then, if you cannot pay the note, once you have paid what
you can, you will not be able to pay the rent. Consider this
your notice that I am commencing eviction actions against you
per the terms of your lease."

"You cannot do this. You are a child," Mr. DeLuca said,
but there was no resolve in his voice. He had no fight left.

Toning down my predatory posture, I said in a more
business-like tone, "Call the SBF offices, call the Realty office,
or call your lawyer. I assure you, Mr. Deluca, I can and will
do this."

Mr. DeLuca sat quietly for what seemed like hours but
was really only a moment.

"There must be some way to avoid this. What do you
want of me?"

Leaning back in his chair and allowing myself to relax, I
told him, "First, I want to know what you have against
teachers."

Mr. DeLuca shook his head slowly. "No, that I will not
discuss. Suffice it to say I have my reasons, personal reasons. If
that is your offer, evict me then."

He surprised me. I'd expected a rant about how a
teacher had treated him unfairly or spanked him too

enthusiastically or something. A refusal to discuss it followed by a welling of tears I had not expected.

"No, Mr. DeLuca, I won't evict you for that alone, though perhaps I should. You see, my wife was one of those teachers you so thoroughly insulted."

Mr. DeLuca looked at me in a different way. Something in his demeanor changed.

"Mr. Lanier, I did not realize you interfered as a question of honor. I thought you were butting in where you had no business. Please accept my apologies to you and your bride."

He stared into his lap for a moment, almost as if he was praying. With a deep sigh he looked up. "Let me tell you a story.

"Fifteen years ago, before I lived in North Carolina, my wife Carlita and I had a son. He was a beautiful baby boy. We thought he was perfect. But there had been complications during the delivery which, while not terrible, caused him to be a little slow to learn.

"We loved Dominick, and it never seemed to us that there was a problem. Then he started school. We tried to tell the teachers that he just needed a little more time, a little more direction, to be able to do the things they were supposed to teach him.

"'No,' they said. 'He was slow. He was stupid.'

"They didn't want to take the time. But my wife took the time. Dommie would come home from school each day in tears. Carlita would sit with him and go over his work. She would find ways to help him understand it. He would regain his confidence, only to have it struck down again by the teacher the next day when he couldn't grasp the next thing quickly enough.

"My Carlita tried to talk to the teachers, the principals, but no one would listen, no one would help.

"Three years ago, after all those years of struggling, I received a call at the restaurant and came home to find Carlita in tears. Our precious boy had killed himself. One week later, Carlita took her own life. It is a wonder that I didn't take mine.

"I blamed his teachers. All his life they had run him down and made him feel worthless. No matter what his mother and I tried to do, they did nothing but hurt him. Do you still wonder why I don't like teachers?

"Eventually, I recovered enough of myself to want to start over. Several months ago I met a woman who began to help my heart heal. She encouraged me to leave that place and come here. She had gone to the university here and told me what a wonderful city this was. So, I came and with the help of…well, I guess with your help though I didn't know it, I was able to start Primavera's. Everything was going wonderfully until today. You see, Mr. Lanier, it was three years ago today that…that…my little boy…"

Mr. DeLuca could not continue the story through his tears. "I should not have come to work today. Linda told me not to. I should have listened to her. Now I am ruined."

His story was tragic. I don't know that it justified how he had acted, but I knew that I wasn't going to put him out of business.

"No, Mr. DeLuca, you are not ruined. I'm very sorry about what happened to your family, but those teachers who failed Dominick were not in your banquet room today. I know those teachers who were in there today, each and every one of them. They are not the unfeeling, uncaring losers who failed your son. They are devoted, dedicated teachers who put their students first. I went to school where they teach. My wife teaches there now. Most of those people are my friends. Mr. DeLuca, they are not the people who hurt you."

"I realize that now. Too late do I realize that," Mr. DeLuca said sadly. "How can I ever make right what I have done this day?"

"Mr. DeLuca, you could apologize to them. If you want, I will talk to them. I won't tell them anymore than you want me to, and then you can apologize."

He looked at me sadly, and asked, "Will that be enough?"

Hoping to lighten his mood, I ventured with a smile, "Maybe a gift certificate for a meal?"

Now Mr. DeLuca smiled too, a wan smile, but a smile. "That I think I can do, yes. Mr. Lanier, thank you."

"Mr. DeLuca, you are welcome. And I apologize for the things I said about you and your restaurant." I rose and came around the desk.

"Nonsense," Mr. DeLuca said, standing also. "It was the shock I needed to make me come around."

We discussed briefly how we could get the staff together for him to offer his apology, and he decided to invite them all to a free New Year's Eve dinner there at the restaurant.

Twelve

I caught up to Maeve and the teachers at Dupree's just as they were being served their pizzas. There didn't seem to be anyone else in the place besides them. That's when I noticed the sign on the door, CLOSED FOR PRIVATE PARTY. Alfred had closed the place down for them. I owed him big time.

"Alfred, I didn't expect you to do that. I'll make it up to you," I said.

Alfred put his arm around my shoulder and laughed, "What, so a few people have to wait to have some of my pizza another day. They'll come back. You don't owe me a thing, Michael. If it wasn't for you, I wouldn't even be here to be closed, if you get my meaning."

I eyed him suspiciously, "What do you mean, if it wasn't for me?"

Shaking his head and clasping his hands in front of him almost as if in prayer, Alfred replied, "Michael, Michael, I talked to you about wanting to open my own place. You say you think it is a good idea and maybe it can happen. Suddenly I hear from some people who want to help me start my own business with terms too good to be true, and it's on the level. I may just be a poor purveyor of pretty good pizza, Michael, but I can put two and two together."

I smiled and shook the hand he held out to me. "Officially, I have no idea what you are talking about. As a friend, thank you again."

Alfred went back to work, and I went to find Maeve. As I walked up to the table, she put a piece of pizza in my mouth.

"Did you tell Alfred to kick everyone out for us?" she asked me with a disapproving frown.

I held up my hands as if warding her off. "All I asked him to do was make up a few extra pizzas. I expected you guys to eat them on the bus."

"On the bus, huh," Maeve said with something between annoyance and amusement. "Well, I'm glad he didn't. We've got to clean that bus out before we give it back."

Turning more serious, she asked, "What happened with DeLuca?"

Taking a deep breath I motioned toward an empty table near the back of the room. "That will take some telling," I said.

Mr. McHale joined us as we sat down, and I told them what I'd learned when I talked to Mr. DeLuca. When I finished, there were tears in Maeve's eyes.

"Michael, may I share that story with my staff?" Mr. McHale asked solemnly.

Nodding slowly, I told Mr. McHale that Mr. DeLuca said it would be all right to tell enough to help them understand why he acted the way he did.

"He also asked that I make sure you all understand how sorry he is for what happened," I added.

Mr. McHale related the story and the apology to the staff. He told them Mr. DeLuca would like to apologize to them all in person and that they had all been invited back for a complimentary New Year's Eve dinner. After some discussion it was decided that they would accept both the apology and the invitation.

Thirteen

My final exams were finally over, and Maeve's first semester as a high school teacher drew to a close. It was time to plan for Christmas. It turned out we didn't have that much to plan. Grandma Lillian had decided she wanted to bring back the tradition of hosting a family Christmas Eve and had convinced my aunt to go along.

Since their house would be a bit small for such a large gathering, the family arranged to have the party in the Berne Restaurant at the corner of Glenn Burnie and Neuse Boulevard in New Bern. The restaurant had a sizable banquet room and a nice buffet. All the family would have to do was show up and enjoy.

That worked out well for Maeve and me since we'd left for River Dream as soon as school was out and planned to stay there until New Year's Eve. We'd be going back to Wilmington for New Year's Eve at Primavera's.

Christmas Eve at the Berne wasn't quite like the ones I remembered as a kid, but the whole family seemed to enjoy themselves at Grandma Lillian's party. When Maeve and I got back to River Dream, after Maeve fell asleep, I slipped out to the living room and put a special present under the tree. Maeve had made me promise not to be as extravagant for Christmas as I had been the year before when I bought her the Porsche. I kept my promise, in terms of dollars anyway.

We slept late Christmas morning. I woke first and was just getting the wood stove started when Maeve, hands wrapped around a cup of tea, settled onto the couch. She smiled when she saw the little Breyer horse under the tree. It looked just like Raven.

"Michael, where did you find it? I love it." She was beaming like a kid.

"I just asked Santa to bring it to you, and there it is," I told her. "You know Santa always comes through."

The toy horse was fully tacked up, and it took her a moment to notice.

"Michael, this saddle is genuine leather," Maeve said as she held it close to her face and took a sniff. She eyed me suspiciously.

With as innocent a smile as I could manage, I told her, "And the fittings are real silver, and the stones are real turquoise."

Her smile faded just a bit as she scolded me. "Michael, I told you not to be extravagant this year."

A guilty smile replaced my innocent one. "Then you'd probably better not read the note wrapped up in the bedroll."

At the back of the saddle was a bedroll, a real wool blanket, with a note rolled up in it. Maeve pulled the note carefully from the roll and read it.

Whatever you do, don't go to the tack room.

Her lips twisted into a puzzled frown. "What does that mean? What's in the tack room?"

I sighed a dramatic sigh. "If you don't want to get mad at me, you probably shouldn't go out there." Then I started to chuckle.

Maeve gave a frustrated laugh. "Come on, Michael, let's get dressed and go out to the tack room."

"Not yet," I said with a mischievous grin. "That was your stocking present. You don't get your other presents until after breakfast."

Having gotten a good fire going in the wood stove, I pulled myself off the floor and headed into the kitchen. I had just gotten my coffee poured when Maeve walked in with an expectant look on her face.

"You are kidding, right? You're not really going to make me wait until after breakfast, are you? I mean, I need to go out and feed Raven anyway."

We'd brought Raven to River Dream the very day we'd gotten home for the break.

Sipping slowly at my coffee, giving the impression I was considering telling her she'd have to wait, I said nothing for a minute. After making a show out of savoring the java, I finally gave in.

"I suppose you are right, you do have to feed Raven anyway, so I guess we can go see what Santa left you in the tack room."

With a look of triumph on her face, Maeve set her mug down on the counter and hurried to the bedroom to change. I followed with a silly smile on my face. I was having way too much fun. A few short minutes later we were dressed in jeans and sweatshirts, heading to our little stable.

I made a big show out of opening the tack room door. As I clicked on the light, Maeve's eyes grew wide and her jaw dropped. There on the saddle rack sat a full-sized, custom-made saddle like the one on the toy horse under the tree.

Hand carved into the leather were a series of orchids like the ones in Maeve's wedding bouquet. The padded, inlaid seat, in the shape of a heart, was the same heather blue as her eyes. Her name was stamped into the back of the cantle in gothic script. The saddle string conchos were silver, accented with turquoise, and hand engraved with images of sailboats.

Maeve looked at it, looked at me, and looked back at it. In a quiet voice she said, "Oh, Michael, it's beautiful."

She walked over to it and lovingly stroked the leather. It took her a moment to notice the matching saddle pad under it and the bridle hanging on the peg behind it.

"Thank you, sweetheart," she said, blinking away the tears forming in her eyes. She walked over to me and put her arms around me. "I love it. It's exactly the one I wanted. How did you know?"

When we bought Raven the summer before, a set of tack had come with her. The saddle wasn't exactly what Maeve wanted, but she insisted it would do until she decided what she did want. Rita helped me figure out what to get her.

Without letting her know why, Rita got Maeve talking about saddles until she had a pretty good idea of what Maeve wanted. Then Rita helped me find someone who could custom make exactly the saddle that would be best for Maeve and Raven. Judging from Maeve's reaction, we'd done well.

"Rita helped a little. Well, maybe more than a little. Okay, Rita helped a lot," I admitted. "I'm glad you like it."

Maeve smiled the sweetest smile at me. "Let's get Raven fed. Then we can get fed and I can come try it out."

Watching Maeve eat her breakfast, I could tell it was all she could do not to wolf down her omelet.

"We can do the dishes later," she said, popping the last corner of her toast in her mouth.

I shook my head and laughed.

"Yes, ma'am," I said as I put our dirty dishes in the sink before hurrying out the back door after Maeve.

Maeve turned Raven out into the paddock before going into the tack room for a closer inspection of her new gear. She went over each piece with great care, ensuring that she knew just how it all fit together.

"All right," Maeve said, turning to me with a smile that crinkled the corners of her sparkling blue eyes. "It's time to saddle up and see how Raven likes her new tack."

Maeve alternately walked and trotted Raven around the paddock, stopping now and then to tighten a strap or adjust the reins.

"You look great up there," I called out to her. "That saddle looks great against Raven's coat."

Maeve's only answer was a widening of the smile that hadn't left her face all morning.

She made a couple more circuits around the paddock and then stopped by the gate.

"Open the gate, Michael. I want to give Raven a chance to run."

Once clear of the gate, Maeve put her head down near Raven's neck and gave the powerful little horse just the slightest nudge with her heels. Raven didn't need much encouragement. I stood there in awe as horse and rider galloped down the length of the field, slowing only to turn at the far end, before galloping back.

Maeve's strawberry blond hair flew out behind her like a comet's tail of auburn gold, a striking contrast to Raven's ebony main. Horse and rider melded into one in an exuberance of Christmas morning delight, running through the cold winter air as if they didn't have a care in the world.

Later, after she and Raven had cooled off from their run and Maeve was brushing Raven down, Maeve said, "It's almost as if that saddle were made just for me."

Her eyebrows rose and her lips formed a perfect O.

Slowly, she stopped brushing Raven and turned to me. "Michael, that's not an off-the-rack saddle, is it?"

"Uh, well, no, it's not."

"I should have known," Maeve said with a shake of her head. "You really are something."

After a cold, clear Christmas morning, the rest of that winter break turned out to be warm and somewhat wet. Maeve did get to do a good bit of riding, and we even got in a couple of decent days of sailing. When it was too rainy for either, we enjoyed each other's company in front of the television watching videos on the Curtis-Mathis video player Maeve had given me for Christmas. Fortunately, Bellangia's carried a decent selection of movies on tape for vacationers to rent when they were stuck for something to do on rainy days.

New Year's Eve morning we moved Raven back to her stall at R&R, made sure the boats were secure, and headed back to Wilmington. We would spend New Year's Eve at Primavera's and the first day of 1985 at home. Maeve's first workday would be the day after New Year's Day. Classes didn't start up again for me until two weeks later.

Mr. DeLuca made good on his promise to make New Year's Eve one that the teachers he'd invited would never forget. He arranged the private event room as a buffet and open bar for them for the night. Everything on his menu was available to be sampled on the buffet table. His finest wines and beverages were poured all through the night. The band he'd hired to play was more of a small orchestra. When midnight arrived, Maeve and I were dancing in the main dining room, which had been transformed into a ballroom, complete with wooden dance floor.

When Mr. DeLuca's countdown reached midnight, I pulled Maeve close, whispered, "Happy New Year, Babe," and pressed my lips against hers in a kiss that I hoped expressed to her how much I loved her and how much I was looking forward to spending that New Year and every New Year after it with her.

After a wonderful night at Primavera's, Maeve and I rose late and were just sitting down to breakfast when the phone started ringing.

"I wonder who that could be," Maeve snapped.

Thinking to myself that she might be feeling the aftereffects of a bit too much champagne, I rose to answer the jangling instrument.

"Why don't you let the machine get it?" she said, referring to our answering machine.

I shrugged and sat back down. When the caller started leaving a message, I got back up quickly.

"Guten Morgen, Hans," I said in German as I picked up the handset.

"Good morning to you," Hans replied with a little laugh. "Your accent is terrible."

"It's a south German accent," I joked.

"No part of Germany is that far south," Hans pointed out. "How are you this fine New Year's Day?"

I mouthed to Maeve that it was Hans on the phone. She gave me a look that clearly indicated she'd figured that out.

"We're good, Hans. Happy New Year's to you. Did you have a nice Christmas?"

"I did," Hans replied enthusiastically. "And an even better New Year's Eve."

Intrigued, I asked, "Why would that be, I wonder?"

"I asked April to marry me last night, and she said yes."

"You're kidding," I exclaimed. "That's wonderful news. I didn't know you two were that serious."

I looked at Maeve, and she raised her eyebrows in question. I signaled her to wait with an upraised palm.

I could almost hear Hans' smile in his voice. "Oh yes, we've been getting more serious, and last night I popped the question."

Hans was living in Raleigh. April lived in Garner. They'd dated on and off since junior high. Hans brought her to our wedding, and they'd been more on than off since. I wasn't really surprised to hear the news.

"I know it's kind of soon, but have you set a date or anything?"

Hans laughed a tired laugh. "Not yet, no, we haven't talked about that yet. You're only the second person I've told, after my parents. I was going to call you first, but April insisted our parents should be the first to know."

"I'm honored to be in the top two," I told him sincerely. "We'll have to get together and celebrate soon."

I was thinking Maeve and I could throw a party for them here in town. As much as Hans loved the beach and seafood, King Neptune's would be perfect.

"We'd like to come down and visit," Hans said, "maybe next weekend. Will you be around?"

"Just a minute," I said as I covered the mouthpiece. Turning to Maeve I told her, "Hans and April got engaged last night and want to come visit next weekend. Will we be around?"

"Yes," Maeve said emphatically, "for Hans, of course we'll be around."

I smiled and told Hans, "We'll be around, old buddy. Just let us know what time you'll be getting here."

"I'll call later in the week and let you know," Hans said. "I have some more calls to make, Michael. I'll talk to you later."

Smiling and nodding, though I knew he couldn't see it, I replied, "Okay, Hans. Congratulations again, and congratulations to April, too."

Once I hung up, Maeve was all questions. I filled her in as best I could based on what Hans had told me.

"I would like to take them out to celebrate. Maybe invite their folks and mine, see if we can look up some of our friends who might still be around town."

"That is a great idea, Michael," Maeve said, sounding puzzled that I'd thought of it.

I turned my lips down in an exaggerated pout. "I do have them once in a while, you know."

Maeve shook her head and rolled her eyes. "Once in a while, yes, you do."

That weekend we succeeded in surprising Hans and April with a party at the King Neptune. Hans thought it would be a quiet dinner with just the two couples. Instead it was a well attended event including all our parents and several of our closest friends.

"Michael, I should be mad at you," Hans said as he recovered from the shouts of SURPRISE. "But how can I be? Thank you, my friend."

I patted him on the back. "It's the least I could do for my oldest friend."

Hans' face took on a momentarily pained expression. He looked around the room. I knew what he was thinking. Rhiannon wasn't there. Neither of us said anything. We'd known each other long enough and well enough that we didn't have to.

April reacted with delight. "Oh, you guys, this is great. We weren't expecting this."

She and Hans moved into the room to greet everyone and be congratulated over and over again. The wait staff brought out drinks, and we toasted to love and success for the newly engaged couple.

We didn't see much of Hans and April for several weeks. They did come and spend one weekend at River Dream, and we did go up and spend a weekend in Raleigh. Along about the third week of February, they called and asked, or should I say insisted, that we be in town over the weekend.

Hans told me, "April was planning a special lunch for some of her girl friends. She wants to talk to them about the wedding."

While April and the girls were having their lunch Hans and I were out on Lumina Pier pretending to fish. It was an uncharacteristically warm day for late February - nearly sixty degrees - and not much wind. There wasn't much biting either, leaving us plenty of time to talk.

"We've picked a date," Hans said. "We've decided on the third Saturday in May. April was hoping for a June wedding, but the church was already booked."

I set my pole against the rail and picked up my coffee cup. "A May wedding will be nice. Maybe it won't be as hot as it probably would be in June. Is the church here in Wilmington?"

Hans shook his head. "No. We've been going to a church up in Garner. April really likes the pastor there. She's asked him to perform the ceremony."

"Then I'm guessing the reception will be somewhere up there, too."

"There's a hotel a little ways up Highway 70 from the church that has a nice reception hall. Their menu is a bit limited, but it does include the basics-beef, chicken, or seafood."

My coffee cup was empty so I walked over to the trash can and threw it away. Turning back towards the rail, I took a moment to admire the view of Wrightsville Beach stretching out to the north. The calm waves of the ebbing tide rolled carelessly ashore, gently tossing bits of sea shell against the sand in a timeless rhythm that would one day see those shells ground into sand themselves. The air was a clear Carolina blue with hardly a cloud in the sky. I felt a sudden longing to be on a sailboat.

Sitting back down on the bench, I said to Hans, "That menu should cover just about everybody."

Hans shrugged. "I suppose so. The manager we talked to said they could also do vegetarian meals if we needed them. I think April has a cousin who's a vegetarian."

We watched our lines for a while. Hans got a bite. When he reeled it in his big catch turned out to be a pin fish that would fit in the palm of his hand.

"Should I keep him for cut bait?"

"Nah," I said. "Throw him back and let him grow some. We've got plenty of shrimp."

Holding the little fish carefully to avoid the sharp spines on its dorsal fin, Hans removed the hook and dropped the squirming little thing over the side of the pier.

"Well, that was fun," Hans said. He looked sideways at me. "At least I haven't been skunked."

"Day's not over yet," I reminded him. "But right now I think it's time for lunch. How do a couple of hot dogs sound?"

"Sounds good to me," Hans said, hooking his line onto one of the rods eyes and tightening his reel. "Reel in your line and let's go."

The snack bar at the pier wasn't too busy. We got our hot dogs, fries, and sweat tea before taking seats by a window with a view looking south toward the jetty.

Seeing the wetsuit clad surfers, Hans shook his head. "Now that's dedication to a sport. You wouldn't catch me in the water in February."

"Me neither," I agreed. "Then again, I was never much of

a surfer."

Hans laughed. "I've seen you on a surfboard Michael. You're not a surfer at all."

"Maybe not," I said. "Sailing's always been my preferred way to spend time on the water."

"And you are a half-way decent sailor," Hans said. "I'll give you that."

For the next several minutes we concentrated on eating our chili-cheese dogs without spilling any of the generous helping of topping on our clothes. After downing the last bite of his, Hans wiped a dab of chili from his chin and cleared his throat.

"I suppose Maeve will tell you when she gets back, but I don't think April will mind if I tell you first. She's going to ask Maeve to be one of her bridesmaids."

My eyes widened in surprise. "Really. How about that? That's nice of her considering they don't really know each other all that well."

"April thinks of Maeve as a friend," Hans said, "a good friend. And since you're going to be my Best Man, April thought Maeve should be included in the wedding party, too."

I chewed and swallowed my last fry and drained the iced tea from my cup. "I think Maeve will like that. Who are the other bridesmaids going to be?"

Hans chewed on his lower lip. "She's only going to have two. She's asking Beth to be the other one."

I had to ask, even though I thought I knew the answer. "Who's she asking to be her maid-of-honor?"

The look on Hans' face told me I was right. "She asked Rhiannon, didn't she? That makes sense. They've been friends practically their whole lives."

Fourteen

Hans raised his eyes slowly and met mine. "April did ask Rhiannon, but Rhiannon said no."

My feelings moved quickly from surprise to relief to irritation. "She said no. What's her excuse? April is one of her best friends."

"From what April told me, Rhiannon's first question when April asked her was if you were going to be there. When April told her you were, she asked if your wife was going to be there. April told her that she planned to ask Maeve to be a bridesmaid."

Shaking my head, I said, "I can imagine what Rhiannon said to that."

Hans snorted. "Yeah, I bet you can. Anyway, Rhiannon asked when the wedding was going to be. When April told her, Rhiannon said she couldn't because she'd already made plans to be visiting friends in Africa the last two weeks of May."

I sat up and swirled the remnants of ice around the bottom of my cup. "Rhiannon's going back to Africa. Do you believe that?"

"April doesn't believe it, but she didn't press Rhiannon about it." Hans tilted his head and looked hard at me. "April doesn't think Rhiannon's gotten over the fact that you married someone else, Michael. And that's why Rhiannon won't come to our wedding, because you'll be there with Maeve."

I felt bad for April, and for Hans. Hans and Rhiannon had been friends as long as he and I had.

"I'm sorry, Hans. Tell April I'm sorry that Rhiannon feels that way."

Hans reached across the table and put a hand on my shoulder. "April doesn't blame you, Michael. She knows it's Rhiannon's issue to deal with, not yours. And, besides, she's already found someone else to be her maid-of-honor. You remember her college roommate, Theresa."

"That makes sense. They roomed together right from fall semester, freshman year."

"Theresa is April's sorority sister. April always said Theresa was like the real sister she never had," Hans said. "She was going to ask her to be a bridesmaid with Beth and Maeve. I guess this works out better."

Theresa, the moms, and the bridesmaids got together and held a surprise bridal shower for April in, aptly enough, late April. The groomsman and I had a bachelor party for Hans the Saturday before the wedding. This was at his request since he wanted his party at Wrightsville Beach and the wedding was going to be in Garner. He didn't want us all to have that long morning-after drive.

The couple opted for a late-morning wedding and a luncheon reception. It was a beautiful ceremony and a wonderful reception. The newlyweds departed late in the afternoon to catch a flight to their honeymoon destination, Lake Geneva, Switzerland.

Maeve and I, rather than drive all the way to River Dream, stayed at the Hilton where we'd spent our wedding night.

"It's funny when you think about it, isn't it?" Maeve commented. "It hasn't been a year since our wedding, and here we are again, on a wedding night."

I chuckled. "But it's not our wedding night this time," I reminded her.

With a coy look, she said, "We could pretend it is."

Fifteen

Hans' wedding fell right in between my finishing final exams and the end of Maeve's first year as a high school teacher. We celebrated with a two-week-long bareboat sailing charter around the Sea of Cortez, starting and ending in Guaymas, Sonora.

The idea for sailing the Sea of Cortez came from one of my professors, Ned Chelte. Dr. Chelte spent months cruising the waters between Baja and mainland Mexico while studying the Manta Ray for his doctoral thesis. He described the area as a sailing and diving paradise.

Summer ended, school started, and life continued much the same way for the next few years. During football season we made every Laney home game. The rest of the time we spent nearly every weekend at River Dream. Each summer we would plan a couple of weeks of sailing adventure at a different destination that promised much to see and much to learn.

Because I was taking a light course load, it took me five years to graduate with my Bachelor's Degree in Marine Science. Maeve and I celebrated by taking a whole month that summer and traveling to Australia to sail along the Great Barrier Reef. It was during that cruise that we first began seriously talking about starting a family.

"Michael, can you hear that ticking?" Maeve asked as we relaxed in the cockpit of our chartered Beneteau 37.

Concerned that she had noted something wrong with the boat, I perked up and listened intently. "What ticking?"

Maeve laughed lightly at my confusion. "My biological clock is ticking. I think it's time that we started thinking about having a baby."

Annoyed at having been fooled, I asked, "What in the world brought this on all of a sudden?"

Judging by the look on her face, I asked a bit too hastily.

"What do you mean?" Maeve responded, her voice tinged with a trace of her own annoyance. She sat up straight and put her glass on the table. I swallowed hard as she glared at me. "You do want children, don't you?"

"Yes, of course I do," I said quickly. Knowing I had to repair the damage already done, I reached out and gently took her hand. "I guess you just kind of caught me by surprise. My thoughts weren't exactly on the parent track tonight."

Maeve visibly relaxed and leaned closer to me. "No, I don't imagine they were. But when we saw that pod of porpoises with their young today it got me thinking about us having a baby," Maeve said wistfully. "Michael, I would really like for us to have a child."

I slid closer on the seat and put my arm around her. "Babe, I would love for us to have a baby. If you're ready, then I'm ready," I assured her. "In fact, why don't we go below and get started right now?"

"Fresh!" Maeve exclaimed, but she was smiling when she said it. "It won't be quite that easy. I'll make an appointment with my doctor when we get home, before going off the pill.

Then we can start working on a baby."

Hugging her to me gently I said, "All right, that makes sense. We could still go below and practice."

"Yes, we could," Maeve agreed as she stood and reached for my hand.

As it was a couple of weeks before we got back to the States and another couple of weeks before Maeve could get an appointment with her doctor, it was well into the school year before we were able to start working on having a baby. Even then we had to wait until spring to get the good news that we were going to be parents.

We began to suspect it near the end of March. On the first day of spring, the doctor confirmed it. Maeve was pregnant; we were going to have a baby.

"I guess this makes it official, Michael," Maeve said with a warm smile as the doctor told us the news. "We're going to be parents."

"Yes, you are," said the doctor, looking up from her chart. "I'd say you're about seven weeks along."

There was a lightness and joy in my heart like nothing I'd ever felt before. "We're having a baby, sweetheart," I said to Maeve as if she hadn't heard.

Maeve graced me with a tolerant smile. "Yes, Michael, I know."

"You're due near the end of October," the doctor told us.

We left the doctor's office that day with a bag full of brochures and pamphlets. On the way home we stopped by the bookstore to see what sort of books they had for couples about to become parents. Maeve and I were giddy with anticipation. When we got home we couldn't wait to call and tell her parents.

"That's wonderful news," Phyllis said, clearly excited.

"Congratulations to you both. When can we expect to meet our grandchild?"

After getting all the details from Maeve, Phyllis finally put Ted on the phone so he could hear the news from his baby girl himself.

"Yes, Daddy, it's true. Your baby is having a baby," I heard Maeve say. She paused briefly, listening. "Daddy, I'm not much of a little girl anymore." She was quiet for another moment. "Yes, Daddy, I'll always be your baby girl," Maeve said as a tear escaped her eye. "I love you too, Daddy."

Once she got off the phone with her folks, we headed down island to my parents' house to give them the news in person. My parents were thrilled. Malori was ecstatic with the idea of becoming an aunt.

"What wonderful news!" my mother said, in an echo of Phyllis' response. "Now when did you say you were due?"

I sat up a little straighter and said with a touch of pride, "The end of October."

Mom smiled tolerantly at my preening. She turned to my father. "Is that not wonderful, Owen? We are going to be grandparents!"

"And I'm going to be an aunt!" Malori exclaimed. She was practically dancing with excitement and bombarded Maeve with questions.

Now that we were going to going to be parents, we would have to make some adjustments. The Nadeau house, being a three-bedroom house anyway, would require the least amount of work. Maeve had no trouble with the idea of turning my den slash workout room into a nursery.

River Dream would take a little more work. When I designed it, I never thought about the idea of children living there someday, but that day was upon us. Changes would have to be made.

"We could change the office into a nursery," I suggested.

"Then what would we use for an office?" Maeve countered. "I do a lot of work in there on the weekends, Michael. That's where I spend Sunday afternoons grading papers and writing lesson plans while you while away the hours feeding worms to fish."

This was a bit of an exaggeration. I spent almost as much time in the office doing work for the master's degree classes I was taking as she did for the classes she was teaching; however, I'd learned not to take exception to Maeve's occasional forays into hyperbole.

I tried to picture the layout of the house in my mind, something at which I've never been good. My friend Hans could have done it easily enough. That's what made him a good engineer.

"We could build up the back porch screened room into an office," I offered.

"Then where would we grill out?" Maeve asked. "And where would we sit out with our guests to enjoy a nice ice tea on a warm summer evening?"

I started to point out that we also had a screened room on the front of the house and a screened house at the head of the dock but thought better of it.

"What I think, Michael, is that we should just add a room off our bedroom," Maeve said with a sweet smile.

I grimaced as I thought of what that would do to the symmetry I had tried so hard to build into the design, but I bowed to the inevitable. Standing behind her chair, I rubbed her shoulders and kissed her lightly on top of her head.

"Of course you're right, sweetheart," I conceded. "That would be the most practical solution."

The architect who drew up the plans for River Dream was available and soon had plans for the new room drawn up.

The contractor who built the house didn't handle small projects like additions but recommended someone he said would do an excellent job. While I handled that part of the task, Maeve concentrated on planning the interior of the nursery. We were busy with preparations and excited about the adventure of becoming new parents.

Sixteen

Only we didn't. One morning in early May, Maeve woke up with bad cramps and pain.

"Michael!" she cried from her side of the bed, curled into a ball and holding her stomach. "Something's wrong. It hurts so bad."

A cold chill swept over me as I looked at her lying there. Trying to stay calm, I helped Maeve to her feet so she could get to the bathroom. That's when I noticed the blood spots on the sheets.

"You're bleeding, Maeve," I said in a quavering voice. "I think we need to get you to the hospital."

Maeve's body shuddered. She looked up at me, tears filling her eyes, whether from pain or fear I couldn't tell. "Yes," she choked out through clenched teeth. "Right now, Michael."

I helped her lie down on the edge of the bed and dressed as quickly as I could. With fear in our hearts, we rushed to the hospital where we learned the bad news.

"Mr. and Mrs. Lanier," the Emergency Room resident said, "we did everything we could. I'm sorry. We couldn't save your baby."

Maeve had miscarried. We'd lost our child.

I put my arm around Maeve and pulled her close. She buried her head against my chest and sobbed. I stroked her hair as my tears fell, unable to put into words the agony we were feeling in our hearts.

Maeve was moved into a private room shortly after the resident made his sad announcement. Her obstetrician arrived as they were getting her settled in. There in that hospital room, I sat by Maeve's bed and held her hand while the doctor tried to assure us that these things sometimes happen, they were no one's fault, and that there was no reason she could see that we couldn't try again once we were ready.

Maeve and I accepted her assurances stoically. They kept Maeve overnight for observation and let me stay with her. The next morning the doctor told Maeve that she could go home. I contacted the school and told them they needed to arrange a substitute for the rest of the week.

I took Maeve to the house on Wrightsville Beach. She slept most of the day. I kept myself busy cleaning the house, keeping an ear out for Maeve should she need me. The next morning I woke to find Maeve already up and making breakfast in the kitchen.

"You should be in bed," I said, walking up behind her and putting my arms around her.

Maeve leaned her head back against my shoulder. "I want to go home, Michael," she said. "I don't want to stay here right now."

Maeve insisted she was up to the trip, so, after letting her folks and mine know we were going, I took her home to River Dream. That night on the front porch, mugs of hot tea in hand, we talked about what to do next.

"Maeve, if you want to stay here, if you want to go

somewhere, or if you want to go back to your classroom, that is what we'll do," I told her. "Just know how much I love you and that nothing is more important to me than you."

"I know, Michael. I love you, too. It's just that I was so looking forward to becoming a mom," Maeve said, unstoppable tears streaking her cheeks. "I feel like I've failed somehow."

I set my teacup down and put my arm around her. "No, sweetheart, you didn't fail. Nature is cruel sometimes, and there is nothing we can do about it. What we can do is keep loving each other and keep on trying."

"I do love you, Michael, and I do want to have your baby. I know that you'll be a great dad," Maeve said, before she broke down and began to sob.

I held her and whispered loving and reassuring things to her. I held her until her sobs subsided, until she'd cried as many tears as she needed to cry.

She heaved a great sigh, looked up at me, and said, "I'll be all right now, love. Thank you. Thank you for loving me." She smiled through trails of tears mapping the heartbreak on her lovely face.

Gently brushing a tear from her cheek, I promised her, "I will always love you, Maeve. Nothing will ever stop me from loving you."

Seventeen

The next morning dawned clear and cool with a light northwesterly breeze.

Looking out over the Neuse, I said to Maeve, "I think we should take *Riverscape* out for a sail. Some time on the water would do us good."

Having convinced Maeve that a day of sailing was just what we needed, it didn't take me long to rig *Riverscape*. After breakfast, we put the wind to our backs and headed downriver toward Pamlico Sound.

Maeve started near the front of the cockpit, looking out over the river as it rushed by our hull. After a time she moved back beside me. We ran before the wind, leaving our pain and loss behind us. Christopher Cross said it best in his song, "The canvas can do miracles." We found some peace as the wind carried us beyond our tears.

"Michael, we can turn back now," Maeve told me as we passed the mouth of South River. Those were the first words she's said since we'd left the dock. Her face, which had been drawn and creased, was now peaceful and relaxed.

"All right, sweetheart," I said.

We tacked hard about and brought *Riverscape* close hauled on a course for River Dream. Upon arriving home, I helped Maeve up onto the dock. She went on up to the house while I secured *Riverscape*. She was in the kitchen putting water on for tea when I got there.

"What would you like me make you for lunch, sweetheart?" I asked Maeve. "How about some grilled cheese and tomato soup?"

"I think that would be perfect, Michael," Maeve said with a tired smile as she took a seat at the kitchen table.

She was quiet while I prepared lunch. As I set her plate and mug of steaming soup before her, she smiled up at me.

"You take such good care of me, Michael," she said. "Thank you."

"I'll always be here to take care of you, Maeve," I said as I sat down with my lunch. "I love you."

"I know you do, Michael. I love you, too." Maeve took a careful sip of her soup.

"Michael, after lunch I'd like to drive out to the stable," Maeve said. "I'd like to see Raven."

"All right," I said.

I thought seeing Raven might be good for her, so after I cleaned up from lunch we drove the Cherokee to R&R. Rita knew Maeve well enough to know something was wrong as soon as Maeve walked into the barn.

"Maeve," Rita asked her, "is everything all right?"

Maeve just shook her head as she walked by on her way to Raven's stall. I stopped to explain to Rita what had happened.

"Oh, Michael," Rita said. "I'm so sorry."

She went immediately to Maeve's side. Maeve had reached Raven's stall. Raven came to the door and was standing there still and quiet while Maeve stroked her cheek.

It was as though Raven could sense what Maeve was feeling.

"Maeve, honey, I'm so sorry," Rita said as she put her arm around her.

Maeve took a deep breath before replying, "Thank you, Rita."

Later in the week, Maeve felt she was up to some riding and spent some time at the stable with Raven. I went with her the first day to keep an eye on her and make sure she was really up to it. I was being overprotective, but Maeve didn't seem to mind.

The next day she insisted I stay home and get some work done around the house. As there really wasn't anything for me to do, I spent the time working on *Geddaway* instead. I planned on us taking her over to Morehead City for the weekend. On that trip we discussed several things.

Maeve and I decided to postpone our open-water crossing to Bermuda, planned for that summer, until fall. Second, we decided that Maeve was going to take a year off from teaching so we could concentrate on baby making. In conjunction with that, I would take a sabbatical from the university and my master's degree work.

We would spend the summer at River Dream sailing and practicing for the trip to Bermuda. Also, Maeve would get to spend lots of time riding Raven. There was one other important thing we decided. Instead of chartering a boat for the crossing to Bermuda, we decided to buy a bigger boat. *Geddaway* might have been enough of a boat, but I wasn't one to turn down the chance to buy bigger boat!

We returned to Wilmington after our cruise to Morehead City so Maeve could finish out the school year and break the news that she was taking at least a year off. Her principal was sorry to see her go but very understanding about the reasons. As the school year drew to an end, we closed up the Nadeau house and prepared for our longest stay yet at River Dream.

"It's funny, isn't it, Mike? This will be the longest we've ever lived at home," Maeve quipped.

"It is a little ironic, isn't it?" I replied.

Maeve and I settled into life at River Dream. During the week we alternated time between the stables and the boats. Weekends Maeve would go trail riding with her horse friends while I volunteered at camp. Somewhere in between we selected our new boat, a Beneteau 331. It was seven feet longer and broader in the beam than *Geddaway*. It was also roomier below decks. We had chartered an older version of the same boat years earlier on a trip to Greece and liked it very much. It was supposed to arrive in mid-August, and we were anxiously awaiting our first sail on her.

Eighteen

August 5, 1989

It was a warm and hazy Saturday morning that promised to turn into a hot and humid day. Maeve left at sunup to meet her riding club at the stables before they loaded up the horses and headed for the Minnesott ferry landing. They were going on a trail ride over in the Croatan National Forest. An early start was planned so they could be back on the ferry and on their way home before the real heat of the day settled in. I spent the morning doing some of the eternal maintenance that seems to accompany sail boat ownership.

The phone call came just as I sat down to have some lunch. It was my cousin Denise.

"Mike, there's been an accident. Maeve's hurt. She's here at Craven Medical, but the Life Lift chopper is on its way to take her to Pitt."

I staggered against the counter and nearly dropped the phone. Taking a firm grip on the handset, I demanded, "What!?! What happened?"

"Her horse spooked and threw her. She landed wrong. It took rescue crews a while to get to her. We've done everything we can here. We're sending her on to Pitt."

"Is she going to be all right?" I begged, a sick, sinking feeling grasping my heart.

She took several agonizing seconds to answer. "Michael, right now, we just don't know."

Denise was an Emergency Room resident at Craven Medical Center. She'd seen a lot of things on the job. If she was as worried as she sounded, I knew it must be bad.

"Michael, you need to get to Pitt as quickly as you can," Denise insisted. "I'll call your mom and dad. You need to get going now."

One of the things I learned in the Navy was how to compartmentalize my feelings. Right then I had to do just that. I headed out to the airstrip to get the Cessna into the air, stopping only to check that I had the right chart on board for the airport in Greenville. Never once did I stop to think about how I was going to get from the airport to the medical center.

Most of the flight was a blur, but, somehow, I managed to fly the plane to Pitt County Municipal Airfield. Once there, I called a cab to get me to the hospital. The people at the hospital were very helpful and guided me up to the ICU/Trauma unit where they were doing everything they could for Maeve.

The doctor did not have encouraging news. "The type of injury your wife has, Mr. Lanier, I'm not sure how she held on this long."

Feeling a flicker of possibility, I asked anxiously, "Does that mean she has a chance?"

"I can't give you any false hope, Mr. Lanier," the doctor said softly, as if he wished he could say differently. "Your wife is probably going to die."

I swallowed hard and tried to accept what he told me, but I couldn't.

"Can I see her?" I asked.

The doctor looked down at the chart in his hands before raising his head and meeting my eyes again. "She's been drifting in and out of consciousness. I don't know if she'll even know you're there but, yes, you can see her."

"Thank you," I said.

The doctor had the floor nurse show me the room where Maeve was. She was barely recognizable with all the medical wires and tubes attached. I walked to the side of the bed and took her hand. Her eyes fluttered open and she looked at me.

Fighting back tears and determined to will her to live, I could hardly find my voice. Finally, I managed to say, "Hi, baby."

"Mike," she said.

"I'm here, Maeve," I said.

"I'll be gone soon," Maeve said in a voice so soft I barely heard her.

"No," I said, the thought of losing her cutting at my heart like a knife, "you're going to be fine."

"I'm so sorry, Mike," Maeve said, her voice breaking.

"Don't be sorry, baby, it'll be all right," I said, still fighting back the tears welling in my eyes.

"When I'm gone, Mike, promise me," Maeve said.

"You're not going anywhere," I insisted. My vision started to blur.

"Promise me you'll love again," Maeve said.

"I can't promise that, Maeve," I said through the tears I could no longer hold back.

"Promise me, Mike," Maeve begged.

"Maeve, please, don't go, I love you!" I cried.

"Mike, promise me," Maeve pleaded.

It seemed so important to her, how could I not? "I promise."

"I love you, Mike." Maeve said.

"I love you, too, Maeve," I replied, but she was gone.

I stood there holding her hand, stroking her hair, tears falling down my face, waiting for her to open her eyes again. I kept telling her I loved her, that she couldn't leave me, and that I needed her so much.

Gradually it sank in. My Maeve was really gone. I stroked her hair one more time, gently kissed her lips, laid her hand on her chest, turned, and walked out of the room.

All conversation ceased as I walked into the small waiting room. Someone walked in through the other door. She stopped, looked at me, and began walking toward me. I knew my imagination had to be playing tricks on me.

Nineteen

"Michael, my Michael, I am so, so sorry," Rhiannon said, with tears in her eyes.

I knew I was imagining her. She couldn't really be there.

"How…what…you…" I stammered through my emotional haze.

Rhiannon took a deep breath to steady herself. "I promised you a long time ago, Michael, that if you ever needed me again I would be here. I promised I would not fail you again."

I broke down. "She's gone, Rhiannon. Maeve is gone."

Rhiannon put her arm around me and guided me to a quiet corner where she stayed with me and held me as I was wracked with sobs and grief.

"It's okay to cry, Mike. It's okay," Rhiannon whispered to me. "I know how much you must be hurting. I'm hurting for you. I'm here for as long as you need me."

Finally, after I don't know how long, I pulled myself together. The pain was still intense inside me. I felt like I was going to be sick. I called on all my training and self-discipline to force myself into some semblance of normal behavior.

From somewhere, Rhiannon produced a box of tissue, and I did my best to clean myself up. I still couldn't believe she was there.

"How are you here? I mean, I don't understand," I said.

"Beth called me," Rhiannon said as she wiped her eyes. "When your folks called Hans, he called Beth, and she called me."

"But how did you get…here?" I asked, still confused.

"I live here now, in Greenville," Rhiannon explained. "I'd just gotten home from the supermarket when the phone rang. I let my answering machine get it since I had my arms full of grocery bags. I dropped everything when I heard Beth say it was about you and it was an emergency."

Rhiannon looked at me, and in her eyes I could see remnants of the panic she must have felt.

"So I grabbed the phone and asked Beth what happened. She told me that Maeve was in an accident and was being airlifted to Pitt."

Rhiannon's voice caught. She turned her head and dried her eyes. After a deep, shaky breath, she turned back to me.

"Beth said your folks were on their way. Beth and Hans, too. But since I was right here in Greenville, would I please come."

Her lips quivered, and this time Rhiannon couldn't hold back the tears. "I told her of course I'd come."

She squeezed my hands, took another deep breath, and said, "I prayed all the way over that Maeve would be all right, Michael. I prayed to God that she would be all right."

I took a moment to try to digest the fact that somehow Maeve was gone and Rhiannon was there. Suddenly I was angry. I pulled my hands away and leapt to my feet.

"What spooked that damn horse?" I asked furiously. Rhiannon looked at me, startled.

"Is that what happened?" she asked.

"That's what I was told. She went on a trail ride this morning with her friends from the club. Something spooked her horse, she fell, and now she's gone," I said with rising anger. "I'm going to shoot that horse."

"Michael," Rhiannon said sharply, "is that what Maeve would want?"

"Maeve is dead," I said coldly. "I want that horse dead, too."

But Maeve had loved that horse. She was a good horse. She would follow Maeve around the paddock like a puppy. I could never hurt that horse.

"Listen to me. Maeve would be ashamed of me." I thought I was going to start crying again. "I can't do this."

"You can't do what, Mike?" Rhiannon asked, concern in her voice. She was gently rubbing my back like I was an upset child she was trying to comfort.

I shook my head in confusion. "I don't even know. I don't know what to do now. What am I supposed to do now?"

"You take it one second at a time. Then the seconds become minutes and eventually the minutes become hours. After a while you go almost whole days without thinking about what you've lost," Rhiannon said.

I stopped and looked at Rhiannon, really looked at her. There were tears in her eyes, and pain.

"You've been through this, haven't you?" I asked gently. I didn't realize then that she was talking about losing me.

"No, not this I haven't. Not what you're going through here. But yes, I know what it's like to feel the pain of losing someone and living with that every day," Rhiannon said, remembering the day she watched my wedding from that fourth floor window. "But right now you have to face some people. Your parents are here."

She took me by the arm and helped me to my feet as mom and dad walked over.

"Oh, Michael, I am so sorry. I just cannot believe this. I am so sorry." My mother sobbed as she took me in her arms.

My dad stood behind her and put his hand on my shoulder. I saw Rhiannon quietly make her way to the door. She looked back at me, mouthed "I'll be back" and slipped out.

I told my mom and dad what I knew of what happened. I filled them in on what took place when I arrived at the hospital in Greenville; how I had been with Maeve when she died.

While we were talking, Hans and April came in. When they found out Maeve was gone, Hans took me in a bear hug while April wept quietly beside him.

The floor nurse came out to tell me that if I was up to it she had some things they needed to discuss with me. My dad stepped up and told me he'd take care of it.

I squared my shoulders and said, "I need to do it, Dad. It's my responsibility."

He held my arm. "You're right, it is. But that doesn't mean you have to do it alone. I'm coming with you."

"Okay, Dad," I said, feeling some of the weight come off my chest. "Thank you."

We took care of the paperwork and I made the necessary decisions. Maeve would be taken home to River Dream and laid to rest in a corner of the property we'd set aside for our children to build homes on some day. It wouldn't be needed for that now.

Twenty

Maeve's mother and father arrived at the hospital shortly after my father and I finished making the arrangements for Maeve to be taken home to River Dream. Cynthia followed closely behind them. They sat with my parents and me in the waiting room as my father explained what had happened. Maeve's mom and dad clung to each other while Cynthia sobbed quietly in a chair next to them.

I couldn't bring myself to look at them. They'd trusted me to take care of their little girl, Cynthia's baby sister, and I'd failed. Shame added itself to the list of painful emotions tearing me apart.

Finally steeling myself to meet Ted's eyes, instead of the shared grief I expected to see, I saw only anger. I lowered my eyes. Ted and Phyllis left without speaking to me.

Cynthia was kinder. "Michael, they're upset, angry, and in pain. Mom and Dad know this wasn't your fault. Give them time."

Her words were spoken kindly, but there was ice in her eyes. She would need some time before she stopped blaming me, too.

When I got back to River Dream the day after Maeve's accident, I couldn't bring myself to sleep in the house, so I slept aboard *Geddaway* instead. I slept there each night until the funeral. Mom, Dad, and Malori came to River Dream late on the day I returned and stayed in the house.

That first night back, Malori sat out on the dock with me until the wee hours sharing stories about Maeve. We probably would have stayed up all night if Mom hadn't insisted Malori go inside and get some sleep.

Maeve's funeral was held two days after the accident in an historic little church on the property at River Dream. Then I laid her to rest on a rise of land with a view of the river. I knew she'd like that spot.

Our friends and family gathered at the house afterward. Most stayed for only a brief time before offering one last condolence, taking their leave, and going on their way. I did my best to be patient with them. I knew they all meant well. I just wished they'd go. I wanted to be alone, or at least I thought I did.

When the funeral was over and most of the mourners were gone, only my closest family and friends remained. Derrick and his family had a long drive back to the Outer Banks and were the first of this last group to leave. Chase and his wife followed them soon after. Beth left with Hans and April. They had all come down from Raleigh together.

The hardest parting for me had been Maeve's folks. They managed to be civil with me but were obviously still blaming me for Maeve's death. It hurt that they shut me out so, not grieving with me. When they left, it felt so final, like I'd never see them again.

Mom, Dad, and Malori left - they'd be staying in Oriental for a couple of days - after assuring themselves that I would be okay by myself for the night.

"Michael," my mom said, "if you want us to stay, or your dad to stay, we will stay."

"Thanks, Mom," I said, after thinking about it. "I'll be all right. I have to get used to it eventually. I might as well start tonight."

My dad looked worried at the idea of leaving me there alone. "You don't have to rush it, son."

I was tempted to ask him to stay. I took a deep breath to give myself a moment to collect my thoughts.

"It'll be okay, Dad," I said. "Thanks."

Rhiannon remained behind. After Mom and Dad left, I found Rhiannon standing on the front porch looking over the river. The sun was setting off to the southwest, and the sky was a blaze of color. She didn't turn as she heard me walk up.

"I'd forgotten how beautiful it is here, Michael."

At that moment I couldn't see the beauty anymore.

"Somehow I don't think I'll ever look at it like I used to," I said. "I've lost everything that made this place home to me."

For a time we didn't say anything. We just watched the light leave the sky.

As the river became dark, Rhiannon turned to ask me, "What will you do now, Mike?"

"I don't know. I haven't thought that far ahead. I'm still taking it one second at a time."

Taking hold of my arm and turning me so that I faced her, Rhiannon assured me, "You may not believe it now, Michael, but you will be okay."

Taking a deep breath, I replied, "I know. I just wish I knew when."

"I don't have to leave tonight, Michael, if you want some company," Rhiannon offered.

"Thanks," I said, "but I'll be all right."

She nodded slowly and released my arm. "Then I guess

I'll go. If you need anything, or just want to talk, you'll call me, right?"

I turned back to look out over the dark, empty river, as dark and empty as my heart. Then I turned back to Rhiannon. "If I do, I will, I promise."

"I mean it, Mike. Tonight, tomorrow, a year from now, you call me if you need me," Rhiannon said, lowering her chin and raising her eyebrows in emphasis. Suddenly she was that best friend I knew from days gone by, knowing what was good for me better than I did myself, and not shy about reminding me.

"I will, Rhi. We may have forgotten for a while, but you're still my best friend."

"You haven't called me Rhi since we were five," Rhiannon said with a slight smile.

"Thanks for being there, Rhiannon. I would have fallen apart if you hadn't walked in that door." I struggled to keep my voice even.

"I let you down once, Michael. I'll never let that happen again, that you can count on." She gave me a quick hug, walked to her car, and drove off. I was alone with my memories.

I stood there on the porch in the deepening dark for some time. Then I turned and went into the house. *Geddaway* would be unoccupied tonight. It was time I faced my ghost.

Twenty-one

The next day I woke up alone in our big empty bed in our big empty house and realized that, without Maeve, it no longer felt like home. Without her, it was just a place to stay. A place that maybe I needed to get away from for a while, maybe for a long while. I knew that someday I might be able to return, but right then I just didn't want to be there.

Having decided I didn't want to stay at River Dream raised the question about where to go. I decided to go sailing. Sailing had always been my way to escape.

Since it was August, I figured I'd sail south for the fall. I'd spend the winter among the islands and in the spring, well, I'd decide then where to go next.

Maeve and I had been planning that trip to Bermuda, so we'd been taking navigation classes and had ordered the new boat. It was due to be delivered the next week, giving me time to get myself ready to go and time to get River Dream ready for me to be gone. The first thing I did was call my father.

He sounded skeptical. "So you've decided to go sailing. You're going to spend the winter sailing the Caribbean."

Knowing my dad, I should have expected that.

"Yes, that's what I'm thinking," I said. "The new boat will be ready on the sixteenth. I just need to make arrangements for someone to look after River Dream while I'm gone."

There was a moment's pause.

"Just how long do you think you will be gone?" my father wanted to know.

How long I would be gone was something at which I could only guess. "Six months, a year, it depends."

"You're going to go off sailing around the Caribbean for a year?" my dad asked. He no longer sounded skeptical, but his voice wasn't approving either.

"You sound like you think it's a bad idea," I said a bit defensively.

"No, not at all, I'd love to go with you," Dad said.

In the background I heard my Mother say, "I heard that, Owen."

Dad chuckled at my Mom's remark. "All right son, I'll make a few calls and get things set up with the house. What about the other boats?"

I hadn't thought about that. The other boats couldn't just sit at the dock at River Dream indefinitely.

"I'll get Jeremy to store them for me. I'm sure he won't mind the rent money."

"Son, he probably won't charge you any rent. You own forty percent of the marina, remember?"

"Oh yeah, I forgot," I said sheepishly. "Thanks, Dad."

My next call was to Hans to see if he wanted to come down that weekend and help me sail *Riverscape* and *Geddaway* up to Oriental. Even over the phone I could sense the conflict he felt.

"I would if I could, Michael," Hans explained, "but

April's family is having their annual reunion this weekend. I wouldn't hear the end of it if we didn't go. Her parents are hosting it this year. I am sorry."

"I understand," I assured him, though I was a little disappointed. I wondered whatever happened to anytime 24/7/365. Marriage happened, I guess. The disappointment must have shown in my voice.

"Michael," Hans said, "let me talk to April, explain the situation. I'm sure she'll understand."

Now I felt like a jerk. I should have known Hans wouldn't let me down. It was my turn to be the stand-up guy.

"Really, Hans," I said, "it's all right. I'll call Chase. He always jumps at a chance to go sailing."

"Are you sure, Michael?" Hans asked, concern evident in his tone.

"I'm sure, buddy, but thanks," I said. "Give April a hug for me."

Chase couldn't make it either. He was leaving Friday afternoon for some kind of technology instructors' conference, and the ticket and room were already paid for. He offered to blow it off anyway, but I told him not to do that. Derrick was out of state on a trip with his family. A sad coincidence, but they had another funeral to attend. That's why he'd had to leave so quickly the day of Maeve's service.

I was trying to think of who else might want to do some sailing when the phone rang. Thinking it was probably my dad, I picked it up.

"Hello."

"Hi, Mike," Rhiannon said, her voice tinged with worry. "I called to see how you were holding up."

I took a deep breath and considered my answer. "I've pushed out to several seconds at a time," I told her.

"That's good," she said, sounding a bit relieved.

"Rhiannon, I'm glad you called. Do you still sail?"

"I haven't for a while, why?" she replied, evidently puzzled by such a question.

"I need to sail my boats up to the marina in Oriental this weekend so Jeremy can put them in storage for me," I explained.

She didn't say anything for a minute, and then asked slowly, "Why would you do that?"

"I'm going to go away for a while. Maeve…Maeve and I bought a new boat, a bigger boat. We were going to sail it across to Bermuda and back this fall. I've decided to sail it down to the Bahamas instead and spend the winter bumming around the islands. It'll do me good to get away from here for a while."

"That actually sounds like a great idea. I think it'll do you a world of good. I guess I could come down and help," Rhiannon said. I could almost hear the relieved smile on her face.

"Great," I said. "When can you get here?"

"What time did you want to get started?"

I thought about that quickly and replied, "The earlier the better."

"I could come down Friday after work. Would you be okay with me staying in the front bedroom?"

When she asked, I could almost hear my mother's voice questioning if it was a good idea. I decided there was no harm in an old friend spending the night in the spare bedroom. Any romantic ties between Rhiannon and me had been severed long ago.

"That would be fine with me," I assured her. "I'll see you Friday night."

After getting off the phone with Rhiannon, I went out to the garage to get the Grand Cherokee. As I opened the garage door, I noticed the empty spot where Maeve's car should be. It hit me that her car was still parked down at the stables. For the first time since the hospital I thought of Raven, her mare. I would have to do something about Raven.

Dimly, I remembered Maeve's friends from the horse club at the funeral. They had been very upset about what had happened and very sorry they hadn't been able to do more for her. I mouthed what now sounded in my mind like clichéd platitudes.

Maeve had become close to them but I'd never gotten to know them that well. Now I would need their help finding a home for Raven. I hoped I hadn't been too much of a jerk at the funeral.

Deciding that dealing with that could wait, I backed the Cherokee out of the garage and headed toward Oriental. Then I realized I needed to make arrangements for the Jeep and Maeve's car, too. For a minute I felt overwhelmed. I pulled over, took a deep breath, told myself to take care of one thing at a time, and continued on to Oriental.

"Hey, Mike. I was really sorry to hear about Maeve. How are you holding up?" Jeremy asked when I walked into his office at the marina.

"I'm making it through one minute at a time right now, Jeremy."

Jeremy nodded understandingly. "Just let me know if there's anything I can do."

"Thanks, Jeremy. As a matter of fact, there is something I need to talk to you about. I'm going to need to store my boats for a while."

Jeremy turned around and grabbed a notebook off the shelf behind his desk before he answered. "Not a problem, Mike. I assume you're talking about dry storage."

"Yeah. I'm going to bring them up this weekend. I plan

to make a day of it."

"Do you need anyone to crew for you?" Jeremy asked as he made a note on the schedule.

"No, I've got a friend coming to help out. Thanks anyway. I will need someone to shuttle me back and forth to the house," I said, after a moment's thought.

"I can get one of the guys to do that," Jeremy said. "Your new boat is coming in on the sixteenth. Do you want to store that one too?"

I turned to look out the window that opened onto the boat yard as if expecting to see the new boat sitting there.

"No, that one is the reason I'm storing the others," I explained. "I plan to sail the new boat to the Islands for the winter and spend some time down Bahama way."

Following my gaze, Jeremy said, "That sounds like a good plan. It'll get you away from here for a while. That's probably the best thing for you."

"Yeah, I hope it'll do me some good."

With that worked out, I headed to Scoops to get some lunch. The folks who worked there had known Maeve pretty well, and they all expressed their condolences. When I finished lunch, I knew it was time to head to the stable. I had an idea about what to do about Raven.

Twenty-two

I'd learned that on the day of Maeve's accident, Raven had been spooked by a couple of kids on dirt bikes who weren't even supposed to be in the woods. The kids came around a bend in the trail and practically ran into the horses. Maeve and Raven were in the lead. Raven reared up in fear and surprise. Maeve, who had turned around to say something to the rider behind her – probably about there being motorbikes on the trail - was caught off balance and thrown from the saddle. The park rangers never caught the kids. After learning the whole story, I realized I'd been wrong to put the blame on Raven.

Pulling into the parking lot at the stable, I spotted Maeve's Porsche where she'd left it the morning of the accident. It was kind of hard to miss a red Porsche 944.

For a moment I couldn't breathe, and tears pooled in my eyes. Memories of the Christmas Eve I gave her the car came flooding back. I nearly turned around to leave but, with great effort, got my emotions under control and pulled in next to the Porsche.

I went into the barn to find Rita, the owner. She was

talking to someone, so I headed to Raven's stall. It was empty. I went out the back to look at the paddock, and there she was, grazing. I called to her, and she looked up. A lump formed in my throat. If it had been Maeve calling her, Raven would have trotted right over. My confidence that I could handle taking care of her wavered.

"Mike, we're all so very sorry about Maeve," Rita said as she walked up behind me. She'd probably told me the same thing at the funeral, but I barely remembered seeing her and her daughter there, much less what they might have said.

I swallowed hard, trying to force down the lump in my throat. I finally managed to say, "Thank you, Rita."

"Have you even begun thinking about what to do about Raven?" Rita asked. I suspected she knew that was why I was there.

Turning towards her, I said, "I was hoping you could help me with that. I want to be sure she goes to someone who will take as good a care of her as Maeve did."

I saw tears well up in Rita's eyes.

"Mike, I've always been fond of Raven," Rita revealed. "My daughter is just old enough for her own horse now. I know Raven is a good and gentle horse. If you're all right with it, I'd like to buy Raven for her."

Fighting to hold back my own tears, I reached out and put my hand on her shoulder. "Rita, thank you, I'd like that. I think Maeve would have liked that. But let it be a gift. You don't have to buy Raven. Knowing you'll be caring for her is enough for me."

Now her tears began to flow freely. "I don't know what to say, Mike. Thank you."

We stood there for several moments in shared grief. Finally I pulled myself together and pushed on to the other topic that needed to be addressed.

"Now, about Maeve's car. I'll have someone come by and pick it up this week. I'm probably going to give it to the Community College. They can sell it or auction it off for their Foundation."

"That would be a nice gesture, Mike," Rita said.

"Yeah, well, I don't think I could ever drive it," I thought out loud. I could feel myself starting to tear up again. "God, I miss her so much. I look at that car and expect the door to open and Maeve to jump out and say, 'Hi, honey, what are you doing here?'"

Rita put her hand gently on my back. "I know how you feel, Mike. It was like that for me when I lost my Ray. I kept looking up when someone walked into the barn, thinking it would be him. Sometimes when I'm really lost in what I'm doing it will still happen."

I'd almost forgotten that Rita had lost Ray to prostate cancer the year before, leaving her to raise their daughter while trying to keep up the stable. The stubborn cuss wouldn't go to the doctor until it was too late for them to do anything for him. After that happened, Maeve insisted I go and get checked.

"When does the pain stop, Rita?" I asked.

Rita sighed a mournful sigh. "It doesn't hurt as much as it did," she said sadly. "I suspect it will hurt a little less as time goes by."

"How did you make it through those first days?" I was desperate to know.

"I knew that Ray would expect me to be strong, to go on with my work, to be strong for our daughter, Jacqueline."

Swallowing hard, determined not to let the tears start again, I told her, "I've got no one to be strong for."

"You've got to be strong, Mike, to honor Maeve's memory. She wouldn't want you to up and quit," Rita said, almost scolded.

I realized she was right. Maeve would not put up with me wallowing in self-pity. I took a deep breath. There were things I needed to do.

"Thank you, Rita, you're right. You'll see to Raven then, that she'll be taken care of?"

"You know I will, Mike. Jacqueline will take good care of her," Rita promised. Then, in an uncharacteristic gesture, she hugged me. It was an awkward hug, almost as if she weren't used to doing it, but I appreciated the sentiment behind it.

"Okay then. I'd better be going. I'll have someone see to the car," I told her as she pulled away.

On the way home I thought a lot about what to do about Maeve's car. And the more I thought about it, the more I thought I might not get rid of it, at least not right away. When I got home, I called Mr. Cooper at Camp.

"Hello, Michael," Mr. Cooper said when he answered his phone. "How are you, son?"

"I'm making it through a minute at a time, Mr. Cooper," I replied.

"Well, Mike, you know if there's anything I can do to help, all you have to do is ask."

"Yes, sir. Thank you. There is something I wanted to ask," I told him. "Is there anyone over at camp who could give me a ride out to R&R Stables? I need to pick up...pick up Maeve's car."

"Certainly, Mike," Mr. Cooper said. "Larry's leaving for Oriental shortly. I'll ask him to stop by your place on his way."

Larry Jackson was the program director at Camp Riversail. I'd known him since he'd first come to Riversail as a kid.

"Thank you, Mr. Cooper," I said. "Tell Larry thanks for me, too, please."

"I will, Mike. Is there anything else I can do?" He asked.

"No, sir. Not right now," I assured him. "I just need the ride."

"All right, then," Mr. Cooper said. "Remember though, if you need anything, you call. You hear?"

"I will sir. Thank you, again."

A short time later Larry pulled into the driveway at River Dream in a nicely restored 1957 Chevy Bel Air.

"Thanks for the lift, Larry," I said as I climbed in.

Larry smiled and said, "No problem, Mike. All of us at camp were real sorry to hear about Maeve. We're going to miss her."

"Thanks, Larry," I replied. Nothing more was said as we drove to the stable. Larry turned on the radio to the oldies station - what else in a '57 Chevy? I thanked him again when he dropped me at the stable.

"Mike," Rita said, sounding surprised, "I didn't think I'd see you back this soon."

"I changed my mind about Maeve's car. I'm going to hang on to it for a while, I think."

I went over to the car and hesitated a moment before opening the door. Climbing in, I was surrounded by the scent of Maeve's perfume and leather seats. Expecting it to hit me hard, in some odd way it was actually comforting.

I slid the seat back before starting the car and rolling the windows down. Backing out of the parking space, I could almost hear Maeve telling me to be careful with her car. I smiled a sad smile and pulled out onto the highway.

I took it easy at first to get the feel for the way it would handle. I hadn't driven the Porsche much. Eventually I started to put it through its paces. Before I knew it I was at the drawbridge across the Neuse and headed into New Bern. I took Neuse Boulevard up to Glen Bernie then hooked a left, a quick right, and got onto Highway 70.

Once on the highway, I really let the car have its way. It handled like a dream. Traffic was light, and there were no patrolmen in site as I put mile after mile behind me.

Next thing I knew, I was on the outskirts of Kinston and the low gas warning was showing. I pulled into the station at Wyse Fork for a fill-up and then took the back road cross country to pick up Highway 17 north of Pollocksville.

The Porsche took those twists and turns like it was meant for that kind of road. At the junction with Highway 17 I turned left towards New Bern. When I passed the little white church in Rhems I slowed, turned left onto Tuscarora Road, and drove to Grandma Lillian's house.

"Well, well, Michael, what are you doing here?" a surprised Grandma Lillian asked as she answered her door and saw me standing there.

"I was just in the neighborhood, so thought I'd drop in," I said, knowing that she knew better.

Grandma nodded and gestured for me to come inside. "And you happened by just in time for dinner." Noticing the Porsche, she asked, "Isn't that Maeve's car?"

I turned around to look back at the Porsche. "Yes, it is. I picked it up from the stable and just started driving."

"You started driving and wound up here?" Grandma asked with a raised eyebrow.

"It was on the way back from where I wound up, more or less," I replied, trying to smile.

"I see. Well, come in and I'll get you some supper. After all these years, I still cook too much for one," Grandma said.

We went into her house. I took a seat at her dining room table while she made up plates for the two of us. I tried to help. She shooed me out of the kitchen. We didn't say much as we ate, but after the dishes were cleared Grandma refilled our iced teas and we talked.

"Michael, how are you doing, really?" she asked.

Looking down into my glass, I confessed. "I feel like someone tore out my heart and soul and the pain is never going to stop."

"That's about how I felt when your Grandpa Bill died," Grandma shared as she reached over and put her hand on mine.

"How long was it before you stopped missing him?"

Grandma sat up and looked squarely at me. In a soft tone I'd rarely heard her use, she said, "What makes you think I've ever stopped? Michael, I miss him every day. I loved him very much. But I learned to go on without him, just like you will learn to go on without Maeve, as hard as that may be to imagine now. But you will always miss her. I can't tell you that you won't."

I rubbed my hand over my head and tried to absorb her words. "Did you ever love anyone after Grandpa died?"

A sad smile touched Grandma's face. "No, Michael, your Grandpa and I had the privilege of growing old together. I had no interest in finding another man to love."

A hint of anger rose in my mind. "Maeve and I didn't get to grow old together. Now, without her, I don't know that I want to grow old. Part of me wishes I could die right now and be with her again."

"It doesn't work that way, Michael," Grandma said sharply.

Realizing how my outburst must have sounded, I tempered my emotions. "I know. Grandma, I don't mean I'd do anything rash or foolish, I just want to hold her again."

Tears started falling from my eyes.

"Michael, I know you do. I know how much you're hurting right now. I wish I could make it stop for you."

"With her last words, Maeve made me promise her something," I told Grandma Lillian hesitantly.

Leaning toward me, Grandma asked, "What did she make you promise, Michael?"

It was hard to say the words. "She made me promise her that I would love again."

I looked imploringly at my grandmother. "I don't know if I can keep that promise."

"Michael, the pain of your loss is still too fresh. Time really will heal your wounds. Maeve made you promise that because she loved you so much she didn't want you spending the rest of your life without love. I know you don't want to think about it now, but the time will come when you're ready, and you will remember what she made you promise."

I didn't say anything for a long time while I thought about what Grandma Lillian said. Finally I dried my tears, blew my nose, and rose to my feet.

"Thanks, Grandma, not just for dinner, thanks for everything."

Grandma Lillian rose and walked with me to the door. "You are welcome anytime, Michael, anytime, you hear."

"Yes, ma'am. I love you, Grandma." I hugged her gently.

"I love you, too, Michael. You be careful driving home," Grandma cautioned.

When I got home that night, I parked the Porsche in the garage and walked out onto the dock, hit my knees, and prayed. I prayed that God was taking good care of Maeve. I asked him to tell her that I loved her and that I always would no matter what. And I prayed that when the time came I would be able to keep my promise.

I prayed for the strength to make it through tomorrow

and the day after. I prayed that the pain would end. I prayed that Maeve and I would be together again someday.

Then I rose to my feet, walked into the house, got ready for bed, and prayed for sleep.

Twenty-three

Grandma Lillian evidently called my folks to tell them about my visit because my father called on Wednesday to see how I was doing. He mentioned they'd heard I'd picked up Maeve's Porsche.

"Your mom wanted me to let you know we're planning on coming up and helping you around the house this weekend," my dad said.

"Help me do what, exactly?" I asked.

I could picture my father shrugging his shoulders and looking at my mother. "Oh, you know, help you with things."

"Then you'd better bring sleeping bags," I told him. "Rhiannon is coming down to help me sail the boats to Oriental. I already promised her the front bedroom."

My father didn't answer right away. I could tell he'd covered the mouth piece because I could hear his muffled voice telling my mom what I'd said.

The next voice on the phone was my mother's. She wasn't exactly happy with the idea.

"Michael, do you think that is a good idea, Rhiannon coming there right now?"

"I don't know if it's a good idea or not, but I'm not calling her back and telling her not to come. I know we were out of touch for a while, but she is my oldest friend."

"She is also an old girlfriend, Michael," my mother reminded me, the disapproval clear in her voice.

"Mom, that's long in the past. We don't have those feelings for each other anymore," I insisted, glad that she couldn't see me roll my eyes.

"Well, all right," she conceded reluctantly. "But we are still coming up. Malori and I will stay at the Marina in Oriental."

Acknowledging the inevitable, I asked, "What about Dad?"

"He can sleep on your couch," my mother said, in a way that made it a command rather than a suggestion.

Wednesday and Thursday I spent making calls and drawing up plans for my trip. There was a lot of work that needed to be done, arrangements to be made, and paperwork involved to make sure everything would go smoothly. Finally, Friday arrived and with it my guests. My mother, father, and sister arrived first, soon after I had finished breakfast.

"Malori," I greeted her, "I thought you were working at the aquarium this summer."

Malori put her hands on her hips, tilted her head to one side, and pouted just a bit. "I took some time off to help my big brother. Is that okay?" she asked.

Not able to take her posture seriously, I smiled and said, "I suppose I can put up with you for a couple of days."

There was an ulterior motive in her coming along, my mother's. It became apparent when my mother suggested, "Your sister can help you and Rhiannon sail the boats to Oriental."

"I've got a better idea. Mal can pick us up in Oriental and

bring us back between boats," I countered.

My mom rolled her eyes but didn't say anything more.

"What about your fishing boat?" my father asked as he checked the coffee maker. "Are you taking that up tomorrow?"

I had given that some thought and told him my plan. "No, I thought I'd take it up the day I pick up the new boat."

My dad frowned upon finding no coffee made. He started going through the cabinets looking for filters. "Who's going with you to help sail the new boat back here?"

I closed my eyes and rubbed my forehead. "I don't know. I guess I hadn't thought about that. I've not been thinking too clearly lately."

"That's understandable," Dad said while dumping the old grounds into the trash and prepping the machine to make a fresh pot.

Mom had been watching him with patient amusement. When he hit the button to start the brewing cycle, she turned her attention back to me.

"Michael, I know you probably don't want to think about this yet, but what are you going to do with Maeve's things?"

"Actually, I have thought about it," I said slowly. "I was hoping that while y'all are here we can go through her stuff and figure out what to do with it."

"What about Raven?" Malori asked as she sat down at the table. "What will happen to her?"

Malori was an accomplished rider herself, and she had often ridden with Maeve.

"Rita and I talked about that the other day," I told Malori. "Her daughter is old enough for a horse of her own now. Raven would be perfect for her. Rita offered to buy her, but I told her knowing Raven would be well taken care of was enough for me."

"That sounds like an excellent solution," my mother said.

"Rita and Maeve were good friends," Malori added. "I know she'll take good care of Raven."

"What about Maeve's car?" my father asked.

Impatient for his coffee, he'd moved the carafe out from under the drip basket and was holding his cup under it.

Knowing they wouldn't approve, I told them, "Truth is, I've found out I really like driving it. I think I'll keep it."

"But what about your GTO?" Malori asked. I think she was hoping I'd say she could have it.

"I don't know. I could keep them both, I suppose."

"You could," my dad said. His tone suggested I shouldn't.

Looking into my empty coffee mug, I gnawed at my lower lip trying to suppress the pain brought on by what I was about to suggest.

"I guess what I've really got to decide is what to do about all the stuff in her closet. I haven't been able to bring myself to go in there."

My mom and Malori shared a knowing look.

"Malori and I can do that for you, Michael," my mother said with uncharacteristic gentleness.

I'd hoped they might but hadn't wanted to come right out and ask.

"Thank you, Mom. Thank you, Malori," I said, truly grateful.

My father had finally filled his mug.

"Now," he said, "while your mother and Malori take care of things around here, I think you and I will go fishing."

"Fishing?" I asked. Going fishing was the last thing I expected him to say.

"Yes," my father replied assertively. "Your mother and I think it will do you good to get out on the water, and it will give you and me a chance to talk."

When my mother and father were in agreement about something, it was rarely wise to argue with them. Besides, it didn't sound like such a bad idea.

We motored down river toward Oriental, stopping to fish for a while at the mouth of Dawson Creek. There wasn't much biting, so we pulled up anchor and moved farther down river. Somehow, we managed to arrive in Oriental in time for lunch and tied up at the Wharf, a bistro with docks for boating customers. Mom and Malori met us there. I realized it was all part of some master plan, but I didn't mind.

"After lunch, Malori and I are going to check in at the marina," my mother announced while we were waiting for our table to be cleared. "Once we check in, we'll stop by the grocery store to pick up a few things."

"Yeah, Michael," Malori chimed in with a scolding tone. "Your cupboard is bare."

"What have you been eating, Michael?" my mother wanted to know. There was genuine concern in her voice.

It wasn't until they mentioned it that I realized I'd been living on Pop Tarts and Cheerios all week. I hadn't really cared about what I'd been eating.

"That is not exactly a healthy diet," my mom scolded me when I told her. "We will stock you up with some real food."

"Thanks, Mom," I said sincerely.

When we finished lunch, my father and I motored back to River Dream while Mom and Malori checked into the marina. We tied up to the dock and took a walk up to the airstrip to check on the Cessna. It'd been sitting unattended since I flew back from Greenville. I wanted to make sure it was securely tied down in the shelter. Then, for the first time since the funeral, we walked to Maeve's grave.

Guilt rose up in me as we approached the site. "I suppose

I should be ashamed of myself that I haven't been here every day."

"No, you shouldn't," my dad said, putting his hand on my shoulder. "She's not really here after all."

Fighting to hold back tears, I replied, "No, she's not. Not really. While I'm gone someone's going to have to look after this spot, though."

"That's already been taken care of, son," my dad said. "I've found someone who will look after the house and the grounds, including this area."

I could always count on my dad.

"Thanks, Dad," I said.

As I stood there by the grave, I felt sad and lonely but not devastated anymore. I still missed her so much, yet I knew I would be able to keep going without her. Just the day before, I don't know if I could have said that.

"Good-bye, Maeve," I said quietly. "You were the love of my life. I will always love you, and I will always miss you. But I will be okay. Not today, not tomorrow, but in time, I will be okay. And I will keep the promise I made you. Good-bye, my darling."

Then I turned and walked back to the house. It was time to go on living.

Twenty-four

As my father and I approached the house, he nudged me. Looking up at him, I saw he was pointing at the back porch. I turned and looked toward the porch and saw Rhiannon waiting for us. I smiled a weak smile and waved. She waved back and came out to meet us.

"Hi, Uncle Owen. Hi, Mike," Rhiannon said, giving me a brief hug.

"Hello, Rhiannon," my father said, almost formally. "How long have you been here?"

"Not long, Aunt Eunice just got here and told me you guys had probably gone to the hangar to check on the plane. I was on my way to meet you when I saw you coming across the field."

I was very glad she hadn't come and found us. I really needed that moment at the grave site. But now I was glad she was there and told her so.

Rhiannon looked at me carefully. "How are you doing?"

Taking a deep breath before answering, I replied, "Much better; the minutes are starting to add up."

"That's a good sign," she said seriously.

"Why don't we go inside?" my dad suggested, motioning towards the house.

Supper was a simple affair that night, grilled cheese and tomato soup with corn chips. When Rhiannon learned my father would be staying at the house, she tried to get him to take the front bedroom. He wouldn't hear of it.

We all went down to the dock after supper to make sure all was in readiness for the next day's sailing excursions.

"Michael," my mother began, "I still think it would be a good idea if both Malori and Rhiannon accompanied you on board."

I should have known I hadn't heard the last of that idea.

"Yeah, Mike," Malori added, siding with our mother. "Besides, you and I haven't sailed together in forever."

"I agree with Malori and your mom, Michael," Rhiannon said.

I wondered if my mother had spoken to her about it before my father and I got back to the house.

"It will make things easier," Rhiannon continued, "especially with the Hunter. I've never even been aboard her. Have you, Malori?"

Malori shook her head and fixed me with a stare that clearly asked why she hadn't been.

Not only was I overwhelmingly outvoted, but I realized they were right. I was also taken back in time. Memories of the first weekend Rhiannon and I spent together at River Dream, and our first sail together on *Riverscape*, rose in my mind.

Rhiannon had never sailed on *Geddaway*, but she'd spent lots of time on *Riverscape* once upon a time. For a moment I wondered if asking her to come had been such a great idea after all. I decided that having Malori along would be a good idea.

Judging from my father's expression, he agreed with the ladies.

"I hadn't thought about the complications that would arise from having such an inexperienced crew," I said. "Very well, you will both sail with me tomorrow."

My mother shook her head, Malori rolled her eyes, and Rhiannon looked at me with an amused grin.

"What?" I asked her.

A fleeting smile crossed Rhiannon's face. "I just caught a glimpse of the old Michael, that's all," she said so softly that I was the only one who heard her. I wasn't sure how to respond, so I suggested we all go up to the house for some iced tea.

Saturday morning we were all up early. Actually, Mom and Malori woke us up early by showing up to take us to breakfast at the Minnesott Grill. Over breakfast we discussed the final plans for the day's sailing.

There were a couple of young men in the Grill who looked like they might be Marines from Cherry Point. When we walked in, they'd been discussing sailing. After we sat down, they started discussing Malori, not loudly, but loudly enough that I could overhear them.

Even though I still thought of Malori as my kid sister, she was going on eighteen and had grown into a beautiful young lady. She was hot-looking enough to get noticed by the two young men with the GI haircuts. If I'd been in a normal state of mind, I probably would have ignored them. Instead, I rose slowly from my seat and walked over to their table.

Their conversation ceased, and they looked up at me with wry amusement as I approached their table.

"Excuse me, gentlemen. May I ask you to keep your voices down?" I requested politely.

"Up yours, bud," the taller, dark-haired one said. The

shorter guy laughed.

"Get a load a dis guy, would you?" Shorty said, motioning towards me with his thumb.

The tall guy laughed. "Why don't you send that pretty little thing over here?" he said. "Then I could tell her…"

He never finished the sentence. His buddy started to get up and wound up on the floor, stunned, but not really hurt. Tall guy was clawing at my hand in a futile attempt to loosen my grip on his throat. I lifted him from his seat and realized he wasn't that tall after all. When I got him to eye level, his feet were a good three inches off the floor. His eyes began to bug out a little.

"That pretty little thing happens to be my baby sister, you cretin," I said in a calm, even voice. "I would appreciate it if you would be a little more respectful in your admiration of her."

He nodded vigorously to show he understood. Shorty started to stir, so I put my foot on his neck to ensure his continued docility. I stopped applying pressure at a point where he could just barely draw air.

"Now, I think you owe these folks, and the owners of this diner, an apology for your rude behavior, don't you?"

Again, he nodded vigorously.

"I'm glad we understand each other," I told him with a malicious smile. "And to show there are no hard feelings, as soon as you leave, I'll settle your tab."

I gave him a little shove backwards as I dropped him. He landed in his chair and promptly fell over on his back. Then I released his buddy from the floor. He rubbed his throat and climbed slowly to his feet.

"Man, you sure have some moves," Shorty said.

The tall guy pulled himself up off the floor and approached me cautiously.

"What are you, man, Force Recon or something?" he asked, his voice tinged with respect.

Shaking my head, I informed them, "I was Navy, just a boat driver."

Understanding showed in the tall guy's eyes.

"Swick," he said, not as a question, a statement.

"Yeah," I replied.

Shorty looked confused.

"A what?" he asked.

Tall guy ignored him. "My brother was with the boats. I had no idea, man. I'm sorry about those things I said about your sister."

"Don't apologize to me, apologize to her," I told him, indicating our table.

"Folks, miss, we're real sorry for the trouble. We were out of line," the tall guy said.

Shorty, not quite understanding what was going on, wisely chose to echo his friend.

"Yeah, y'all, we didn't mean nothing by it."

The other couple of folks in the Grill just shrugged, told them not to worry about it, and went back to their breakfasts.

"I guess we ought to get going," the tall guy said as he picked up his chair.

Feeling a little guilty, not too guilty, just a little, I asked, "Do you want to finish your breakfast?"

"Well, to tell the truth, I am still pretty hungry," Shorty said with a shrug.

Indicating with a nod of my head that they should sit back down, I told them, "Then go ahead, I'll take care of things with the owner."

I went back to our table and noted that my mother, father, and Malori were all looking at me with something akin to awe. Rhiannon wore a knowing grin.

"Chapter Three, Mike?" she chided me. "Don't mess with my family either?"

Knowing Rhiannon was referring to an incident with our friend Beth's prom date back in high school, I replied, "Something like that," and returned to my seat.

My mother looked from Rhiannon to me and back.

"What does that mean?" she wanted to know.

Looking from my mom to Rhiannon and back, I said, "It's an inside joke, Mom."

Realizing it was all the answer she'd get, my mother pointed out, "That was very noble, Michael, but somewhat foolish. There were two of them."

"I know it was unfair," I said, "only two of them against me and my bionic hip."

Malori was looking at me like she couldn't believe what she'd just seen. She looked over at the two guys, smiled a shy smile, and then turned back to me.

"Michael, that was really something," she said. "What would you have done if one of them tried something?"

I gave her a cold stare and cautioned, "Mal, don't ask questions you don't want to know the answer to."

Secretly, I was relieved those two hadn't tried something. Though I'd kept myself in shape and continued with my workouts over the years, my success was due more to surprise and bravado than anything else.

My father, who appeared to have been made uncomfortable by the whole incident, suggested we put it behind us.

"They apologized and now we're all friends," he said as he picked up his fork. "Let's just finish our breakfast."

Rhiannon wasn't quite finished.

"Malori," she said, "today you joined a very exclusive club."

Clearly puzzled, Malori asked, "What kind of club?"

"A very small club," Rhiannon explained, taking a sip of her coffee. "As far as I know, you and Beth Bosworth are the only members."

Malori was never one to enjoy riddles. "What are you talking about, Rhiannon?" she asked.

"She's just being funny," I said shooting Rhiannon a warning glance. I didn't really mind her telling Malori, but not in front of my folks.

"I'll tell you some day when you're old enough, Malori," Rhiannon said.

Malori looked frustrated but let it rest. My mom and dad looked at each other but said nothing. I dug into my omelet. Rhiannon smiled at me and finished her eggs.

The two guys I'd had the vigorous discussion with came over to apologize again when they left. The tall guy, whose name we learned was Tom, apologized directly to Malori.

Malori replied, rather shyly, "That's okay, Tom. Guys will be guys. I've got a brother. I know how it goes."

After they left, Malori turned to me. "Mike, I almost wish you hadn't beaten them up. The tall one was kind of cute."

"Michael did not beat them up, dear," my mother insisted. "He gave them a stern talking to."

"It sure looked like he kicked their butts to me," our waitress, Judy, said as she came over with our check.

Twenty-five

Deciding to put the Hunter away first was based on the fact that it would take the longest to rig but be the faster boat to sail. We had a pretty good southwest breeze and were able to sail a broad reach until we were just off the harbor in Oriental. There we came about to a beam reach until we had to furl sails and start the motor to navigate into the marina. We'd gone aboard the night before and removed everything except what we absolutely had to have to make the trip.

Jeremy met us at the dock. Once my father arrived and we'd taken the last few things off of *Geddaway,* Jeremy pulled her out of the water to be prepared for long-term storage. Then we went back to River Dream for a late lunch before setting sail in *Riverscape.*

As we made our way downriver in the smaller sailboat, Malori asked, "How long have you had *Riverscape,* Michael?"

I had to stop and think about that. "Since I was seventeen, I guess," I said before easing the sail a bit to take advantage of a puff of stronger wind.

Malori, sensing the change, eased the jib.

"She's in good shape," she commented. "How did you

come up with the name *Riverscape?*"

A sad smile crossed my face at that memory. "I'm sure I've told you the story before."

Malori shook her head. "I don't think so. If you did, I don't remember."

I took a deep breath to get my emotions under control before saying, "Actually, I didn't come up with the name. Maeve did."

When I said that, Rhiannon turned to me with a questioning look on her face.

"I'd forgotten you and Maeve were at camp together," Malori recalled, her interest piqued more by the look Rhiannon gave me than anything else.

The puff of wind passed, and I trimmed the sheet.

"Maeve and I first met at Camp Riversail," I explained. "The summer before my senior year of high school we worked at camp together. My friend, Chase, had a date the day I picked up *Riverscape*, so Maeve volunteered to spend her day off helping me sail her home."

"I thought you never noticed the girls at camp," Rhiannon said with a shake of her head.

"I hadn't until that summer," I replied, and then realized that wasn't true.

There had been one other. I hadn't thought of Christy Ann in years. We'd only been thirteen when we shared our first kiss. I kept that to myself.

Malori checked the jib and decided it was fine.

"So how come you let her name *Riverscape?*" she asked.

I adjusted the tiller just a touch to bring us back to my mark before I replied.

"Technically, I guess she didn't actually come up with the name *Riverscape*. Maeve said something about how the boat would be my way of escaping to the river when I wanted to get away from it all. That gave me the idea for calling her *Riverscape*."

"That's a cool story," Malori said. I think she was glad to see me remembering happy times I spent with Maeve.

Rhiannon, however, seemed a bit perturbed. "Funny how I never heard it," she commented.

"You never asked," I told her.

"So, in all those summers at Camp Riversail, the only girl you ever noticed was Maeve?" Rhiannon asked in a voice strongly indicating she doubted that very much.

I wasn't going to bring up Christy Ann. That would only add pain to the pain I was trying so hard not to feel.

"Yeah," I told her. "Up until then there was a girl back home that had all my attention."

Rhiannon knew exactly who I meant and wisely decided to let the issue drop.

"Who was that, Mike?" Malori asked.

Rhiannon and I both looked at her like she'd just grown another head.

"Oh," she said quietly.

We all kept to our own thoughts the rest of the way to Oriental. By supper time both boats were out of the water and on their way to being ready for some extended time in dry storage. It felt odd not having a sailboat docked at River Dream. I knew it was temporary, but it felt so final.

Between trips to Oriental to pick us up, my mom and dad finished going through Maeve's things, boxing them up for me to decide what to do with them. The things I knew Cynthia or her folks might want, I sent to them. I knew I should have taken the items myself, but I wasn't ready to face them again. It had been hard enough when they came to the hospital and again when I saw them at the funeral.

The rest I told my mother and Malori to go through to

see if there was anything they wanted. For myself, I only kept a few special keepsakes of things Maeve and I had done and places we'd been together.

As evening faded to night, my mother and Malori left for the Marina Hotel in Oriental. My father excused himself to get ready for bed. Rhiannon and I walked down to the dock with some freshly made ice tea.

We sat in the screened room and listened to the crickets, the frogs, and the lapping of the water against the dock pilings. From somewhere in the distance, the thrum of a diesel engine propelling a shrimp boat downriver reached us through the dark night. The west wind brought the faint sound of laughter and singing from a Camp Riversail campfire circle. These were the sounds of night on the river. Their familiar rhythm brought me a semblance of peace.

"Mike, are you still planning on heading to the Islands for the winter?" Rhiannon, stretched out on the chaise lounge, asked.

I was sitting on the swing. "Yes," I replied.

We sat there and listened to the sounds of night on the river.

Rhiannon took a slow sip of her tea. "Mike, when will you come back from the Islands?"

That was something I wasn't thinking about right yet. "I don't know," I said.

We sat there and listened to the sounds of night on the river

Rhiannon thought about that for a moment, then asked, "Mike, will you be visiting your folks in the meantime?"

I hadn't really thought about that either. "Like when?" I asked.

Rhiannon sat up and looked at me. "Like, Christmas, Easter, Malori turns eighteen next spring. Will you come home for things like that?"

Once she mentioned them, I realized I should probably plan on being home for those kinds of things. "I suppose," I answered distractedly.

We sat there and listened to the sounds of night on the river.

Rhiannon relaxed back into her chair. "Mike, if you do come to Wilmington occasionally, maybe we can have lunch or something," she suggested, trying to sound nonchalant.

The suggestion seemed a bit odd, being that she lived in Greenville.

"That would be nice," I said. "But that's a long way for you to come for lunch."

Realizing why I thought that, Rhiannon explained. "Not for much longer. I've applied for a job at UNCW in their admissions office. I got the call this week that the job is mine if I want it."

I wondered about that. She hadn't mentioned anything about it before. Then again, we hadn't really had a chance for small talk.

"That's nice," I said.

"Yeah," she said, "I think so."

If Rhiannon was moving back to Wilmington, she'd need a place to stay.

"Do you have a place to stay?" I asked.

"I thought I would stay with my folks until I found a place," Rhiannon said.

It didn't sound like the idea appealed to her. There was a way I could help with that.

"Could you do me a favor then?"

"For you, Mike, yes, I could do you a favor. What's the favor?"

There was something hard to place in the way she said

that. It had gotten dark and I couldn't see her face, so I couldn't be sure.

"Would you stay in the Nadeau House while I'm gone? That would save you both rent money and having to live with your parents."

Maeve and I had still called the house at Wrightsville Beach the Nadeau House though we'd owned it all these years. It was never home. River Dream had always been our home.

I could tell by the way she hesitated before answering that my suggestion wasn't what she'd been expecting.

"Thank you, Michael," Rhiannon said. "I would be glad to do that for you. But I insist on paying a fair rent."

"Then you can't stay there," I told her.

For a minute she didn't say anything. I think she expected me to say I was joking or something. I wasn't.

"Are you serious, Michael?" she asked, sounding annoyed.

"Yes," I said. I didn't want or need to rent the place out. I did need someone to stay there and look after it while I was gone.

"Why?" she asked.

There were a lot of questions packed into that one word.

Taking a deep breath, I explained. "Because I need someone to stay in the house while I'm gone. If you don't, Malori will somehow convince my folks to convince me to let her, and I don't want her staying in the house."

"Why not?" Rhiannon asked.

Her tone let me know she didn't agree that letting Malori stay in the house was a bad idea. Well, I thought it was a bad idea and told Rhiannon so.

"She's not old enough or mature enough to live there on her own," I said.

"You were living up here by yourself for a good bit of the time when you were her age," Rhiannon reminded me.

"Yeah, I know," I said looking at her with a raised eyebrow. I don't think she could see that, but my voice conveyed my meaning well enough.

"Oh, I see what you mean," Rhiannon said. "What if she lived there with me? I could kind of keep an eye on her. We could be roommates."

It was nice of her to offer, but I couldn't ask her to do that.

"Wouldn't that put a crimp in your love life?" I asked.

"Mike, that is not a worry," Rhiannon said, and then there was a long pause.

I looked toward her, but the silhouette of her profile told me she was looking out at the river.

"Tomorrow we can ask my mom and dad what they think and then talk to Malori," I said. "Besides, she doesn't turn eighteen until next May."

"Okay, Mike, I'll stay in your house," Rhiannon said with a mixture of amusement and resignation.

We sat there and listened to the sounds of the night on the river.

Twenty-six

The next day, over breakfast, I talked to my mom and dad and told them Rhiannon would be moving into the Nadeau House.

My father set down the forkful of eggs that had been halfway to his mouth.

"I thought you were planning to sell it," he said. It didn't sound like he was that keen on the idea of her moving in.

A small burst of anger flared inside me. I don't think I'd ever spoken to my father in a way that dared him to argue with me, until then. "The plan's been changed. Besides, if Malori decides to stay around after college, she'll need a place to live."

My mother set down her tea cup. "Yes, dear, but that is still a couple of years away."

I don't think she liked the idea much either. "I know, but Rhiannon thought that after Malori turns eighteen, maybe she could move in and they could be roommates," I said.

I didn't care much if they liked the idea or not; it was my house, and Rhiannon was my friend.

"That might not be a bad idea," my father said, whether

because he suddenly agreed with me or realized he couldn't convince me otherwise, I couldn't tell.

"Malori effectively has her own apartment now in the loft. I do not see why she would want to move in with Rhiannon," my mother stated.

She was clearly set against the idea. Her gaze traveled from me to my father and back. Then she picked up her tea cup again as if her statement had closed the discussion, and took a sip.

My mother may have thought the discussion was closed, but my father didn't.

"I'm sure you don't, dear. When the time comes, we'll let her decide," he announced.

My father didn't directly contradict my mother very often, but when he did it was final. It appeared he'd come to agree with me.

I let Rhiannon know that when she was ready to move into the house, all she had to do was let my father know and he'd get things set up for her. It was then I realized that the place was still full of mine and Maeve's stuff. When I mentioned this to my father, he said it would be taken care of. We told Malori that Rhiannon was moving into the house. No one mentioned anything about Mal moving in with Rhiannon after Malori turned eighteen.

My mom and dad left after lunch to head back to Wrightsville Beach. Rhiannon left for Greenville shortly thereafter. Malori was going to fly back to Wilmington with me. I would leave the Cessna in the hangar at ILM while I was gone.

Malori had earned her pilot's wings that spring and asked if she could fly us back. Since I'd taught her to fly the Cub years before, I had no qualms about letting her take the controls. She did a good job and put us on the ground in

Wilmington in one piece.

"Have you flown the twin-engine yet?" I asked her, gesturing to the Seneca.

"No," Malori said resignedly. "Dad wants me to wait until I have more single-engine hours."

I was willing to defer to our father's judgment on that.

"I suppose that's not a bad idea," I said. "I wonder if I should even keep it."

Malori looked stricken. "Please keep it, Mike. I'd like to be able to use it after I transfer."

Malori was transferring. This was news to me. "Transfer, where are you transferring to?" I asked. It was the first I'd heard about her wanting to leave UNCW.

Proudly, she explained. "Notre Dame, I've been offered a chance to go to Notre Dame to major in Romance Language Studies. I haven't told anyone…"

Her lip began to quiver and her eyes grew moist. "…anyone but Maeve."

"Maeve never mentioned it to me," I said.

That Malori had shared it with Maeve didn't surprise me. The two of them had become very close. Their common interest in horses had really brought them together. For the first time I began to recognize I wasn't the only one who'd lost someone they loved when Maeve died.

Malori swallowed hard. "I made her swear not to tell until I was ready to tell. I knew if Mom found out, she'd try to stop me. She's gonna have a fit when she finds out."

Malori's lips tightened into a thin line. "Mike, I have to get away from Wilmington."

"I think you underestimate Mom, Malori. If this is what you truly want to do, I think she will back you all the way."

Malori made a face like she just tasted something sour.

"I don't know. She still treats me like a kid," she

complained.

"Sister mine, I hate to tell you this, but you are still a kid," I said with a big brother smirk.

"When you were my age, you were practically on your own and, may I remind you, still in high school. You spent more time at River Dream than you did at home," Malori reasoned. "I'm already in college. Listen, Mike, I love Mom and Dad. I love Wrightsville Beach. But I'd need to get away for a while. This is a great opportunity for me."

Maybe my kid sister wasn't such a kid anymore. "Do you want me to talk to Mom and Dad for you?" I asked.

"No, just be there and be on my side when I tell them tonight," she said.

With a newfound respect for my baby sister, I told her, "That I can do."

That night after supper we sat down in the living room, and Malori announced her plan to transfer from UNCW to Notre Dame that coming spring semester.

Mom was beaming as she exclaimed, "Malori, I think that is wonderful. Why have you not shared this with us earlier?"

I gave Malori an 'I told you so' look.

"I didn't think you'd want me to go," Malori said, somewhat abashed.

A perplexed look crossed our mother's face. "What on Earth made you think that? This is a great opportunity for you. Notre Dame is a fine school."

Malori hadn't expected such a quick victory and didn't quite know what to say. I decided this would be a good time for me to say good-night and headed to the Nadeau house. I parked the GTO in the otherwise empty garage and made my way upstairs. Checking the clock, I decided it wasn't too late and picked up the phone.

"Hello," Rhiannon said with a bit of a yawn.

Thinking maybe it was too late to call after all, I said, "Hi, I didn't wake you, did I?"

"Mike, no, I was just getting ready for bed." Rhiannon said. "I'm surprised to hear from you."

I shifted the phone to my other hand so I could adjust myself into a more comfortable position in the recliner.

"I just wanted to call to tell you some interesting news I heard from Malori tonight."

That piqued her interest. "Really, what kind of news?" Rhiannon asked.

"She's transferring to Notre Dame after this semester," I told her, with just a smidgen of pride.

"Well, how about that," Rhiannon said, sounding surprised and pleased. "Wait, that means she won't be moving into the house with me."

"I guess not," I said, suddenly concerned that Rhiannon might change her mind about staying there.

"Do you still want me to live there then?" Rhiannon asked, sounding like she was afraid I might have changed my mind.

I quickly put that worry to rest. "I would very much like you to still live there, I mean, here. Will you?" I asked her.

"As a favor to you, Michael, I will force myself to accept the offer of your waterfront home to live in. Thank you," Rhiannon said with a laugh.

I laughed too, "Good, that's good."

Changing the subject, Rhiannon asked, "How soon are you leaving for the Islands, Mike?"

Mentally, I thought through all I would have to do before departure.

"The boat arrives Wednesday," I said. "I'd like to take her out and shake her down a few times. I probably won't leave until after Labor Day."

"Then you'll still be around when I move back to Wrightsville Beach," Rhiannon said. The way she said it, it was more of a question than a statement.

"I'll be at River Dream, but if you want help moving I'm sure my dad and I can bring the Suburban to Greenville."

"That would be a big help. Between that and my dad's truck, we should be able to handle my little bit of stuff," Rhiannon said, clearly relieved.

"Just let me know when you need us to come up."

She didn't say anything for several seconds. I started to think we had lost the connection. When she spoke again, it was in a very quiet voice.

"Will you always come when I need you, Michael?" It was almost a plea.

"Yes, Rhiannon, if you need me, I will come," I assured her.

"Thank you, Mike, I'll let you know when I'm ready to move," Rhiannon said in her normal tone.

Twenty-seven

The next morning I got up and worked out for the first time in days. I usually tried to get in some kind of exercise every morning. These weren't quite the vigorous workouts from my high school or Navy days, but they helped keep me in shape. My run-in with those two gents at the Minnesott Grill confirmed that. I followed up with a quick swim off the dock and had just gotten out of the shower when I heard my father come in.

"Hey, Mike, do you have any plans for today?" he asked when I came into the kitchen. He was putting on a fresh pot of coffee.

"I thought I'd go through the stuff here and try to get this place cleaned up some for Rhiannon. Speaking of which, will I be able to borrow the Suburban to help her move?"

"I don't know. Can you drive something that big?" my father joked.

I gave him an exaggerated eye roll and shook my head. "No, I can't," I said. Then I informed him, "That's why you're going to come along, to drive your bus and help move her furniture. She said Uncle Lind was going to go up with his truck."

"That sounds fine, son. I'll be glad to do it." He got himself a mug out of the cabinet and poured himself some coffee. After a tentative sip he turned to me and said, "Now, are you still sure you want to do this trip to the Islands?"

I took my empty mug to the sink and washed it out. "Yes, Dad, I'm sure. Why do you ask?"

He stared into his coffee, his lips pressed tightly together. Finally, my dad took a deep breath and said, "Because I'd like to go with you, at least for the first leg."

I looked at him in surprise. "Dad, I'll be fine. You don't have to do that."

His expression told me I'd misinterpreted his reason for wanting to go. "Oh, I have no doubt you'll be fine, Mike, but I'd really like to go for myself," my dad said. "I talked it over with your mother, and she agrees. I need to get away from here for a while. And I think it'll be good for us, as father and son, to spend some time on the sea together."

The idea made me chuckle. "Dad, first Malori, and now you. Why is everyone so anxious to get away from here?"

My father shrugged as he refilled his mug. Holding the carafe out to me he replied, "I don't know. I just need a little change of scenery to recharge my spiritual batteries, I guess. Besides, I've always wanted to take a slow cruise down the coast. What do you say?"

In response to his unspoken offer to pour me more coffee, I held up my empty mug and then placed it in the strainer. That gave me a few seconds to think over his request to join me on my trip. Surprising myself, I realized I'd be glad for his company.

"I say, welcome aboard. Just remember, on my boat I'm the captain."

He laughed and then suggested that we take *Hey 19* out

for a day of practice. "It's been a while since I trimmed a sail, Mike."

That decided, we headed back to their place, rigged *Hey 19*, and headed out through the inlet to open water.

My dad was a little rusty. Years before, he'd sailed often with Malori, but as she grew older she took *Hey 19* out less and less. Other interests, most specifically horses, had replaced sailing for her. Malori never forgot the promise she made me, though, and kept the boat ship shape all those years. Before we were done for the day, my father was back in the groove. We'd missed lunch, but we didn't care.

When we docked the boat, my father was a little slow climbing onto the dock. I reminded myself that he was fifty-six years old. My father was in great shape, but a long day on the water, when you're not used to it, would wear anyone out.

My mother had evidently been watching for us because by the time we'd secured *Hey 19*, she was coming down the dock with two big glasses of freshly squeezed lemonade. She wouldn't allow powdered drink mix in her house. I don't know why. I loved Kool Aid. It was a taste I developed over many summers at Camp Riversail.

Handing us our drinks, my mother told us, "While you two boys were out sailing up and down the beach like a couple of pirates, Malori and I were working ourselves ragged trying to get your house into decent shape for your guest, Michael."

I took that to mean they'd boxed up all Maeve's things that had been left in the house. "We left you a few things you may need while you are still here. Do you want to look over what we packed up?"

After nearly emptying my lemonade, I replied, "No, I don't think so. Unless you noticed something special, everything I wanted was at River Dream."

"Very well then. You two should go clean up. We, Malori and I, have decided that you are going to treat us to dinner at Primavera's," my mother said. "I am in the mood for something expensive for dinner."

My groan elicited a tight smile from my mother.

I drove to the Nadeau house, cleaned up, and changed clothes. Before long, my mom, dad, and Malori arrived in my mother's new Buick LeSabre. I don't think she'd ever owned any other make or model.

My mother moved to the back with Malori, and I sat in front with my dad. I tried to remember the last time the four of us had gone out to dinner as a family like that, and couldn't.

"Mike, promise me you won't beat up any guys that give me the eye," Malori teased from her seat behind me.

Turning around in the seat, I teased back, "I can't make any promises."

"Michael, you had better behave," Mom warned me with a stern glare.

"Yes, ma'am," I said. I hadn't been to Primavera's in years. I wondered if Mr. DeLuca would remember me.

Twenty-eight

"Michael Lanier, is that you?" a familiar male voice boomed out from behind the hostess station as we walked up to get our name on the waiting list. I looked around and there was Mr. DeLuca, looking a bit older, but a lot happier, than I remembered him.

"Yes, Mr. DeLuca, it's me," I said, stepping over to take his proffered hand. "How have you been?"

"I have been well," he said. Then with concern, he asked, "How are you, Michael? I was very sorry to hear about your lovely wife."

"Thank you, sir," I said, biting my lip and shifting my feet.

Then I remembered that Mr. DeLuca had lost his first wife tragically following the suicide of his son Dominick all those years ago. If anyone understood what I was going through, it would be him.

"You understand how hard such a loss is," I said.

His eyes misted over as he nodded soberly. "Only too well, Michael," he said. "But we must go on, mustn't we?"

"Yes, sir, we must," I said, blinking away the tears

forming in my own eyes.

"Come with me," Mr. DeLuca said, gesturing for us to follow him. "I have a table for you right over here. Tonight's dinner is on me."

His offer took me by surprise. "Mr. DeLuca, that's too kind. You don't have to do that."

Placing his hand on my shoulder, Mr. DeLuca looked me in the eye and said, "Michael, you once did me a great service; this is the least I can do."

It was all I could do to reign in the tears threatening to fall. "Thank you, Mr. DeLuca," I did manage to say, past the lump in my throat.

"I'll get your waitress. Please, enjoy your meal. I will oversee it personally," Mr. DeLuca said.

When he left to find our waitress, my father turned to me. "Michael, I had no idea you knew Mr. DeLuca so well. Or that the two of you were on such good terms. Isn't he the one that year at Christmas…" he said, his voice trailing off.

That was a bittersweet memory. "Yeah, actually, that's when we became, I guess, friends." I said. "It's a long story."

I related to them a carefully edited version of what I had learned from Mr. DeLuca that day. My father knew part of the story, but my mother and Malori were hearing it for the first time.

Her voice breaking with emotion, my mother said, "In all these years we have been coming here, I had no idea."

"Wow, Mike, you sure have a way with people," Malori said in a tone between respect and amusement.

When our waitress took our order, I surprised everyone by ordering the eggplant parmesan.

"Really, Mike," Malori said, "eggplant, since when?"

"Actually," I replied, "I've never had it before. But it's the only thing in the menu I've never tried, so, I'm gonna try it."

Malori ordered the Clams Italiano. Our mother had her usual, Stuffed Shells with meatless marinara. Seven-Layer Lasagna was our father's choice. Between the salad, Italian bread, and our entrées, we ordered our dessert – four slices of Primavera's famous chocolate mousse – to go.

The meal was delicious. Good to his word, Mr. DeLuca did not present us with a bill. I tried to guess what the tab would have been and tipped our server accordingly. We thanked Mr. DeLuca profusely for his kindness. Much to my surprise, he actually hugged me as we left.

"Remember, Michael, your money is no good at Primavera's. When you're in town, you come by anytime. There will always be a table for you."

It was a quiet ride home. When they dropped me off at the house, my dad and I set a time for me to go by his place and pick him up in the morning. We'd be driving up to River Dream in the GTO, and I wanted to get an early start. There were some things I needed to get done before the new boat arrived.

Twenty-nine

When my dad and I got to New Bern the next morning, I realized I hadn't been thinking very clearly in bringing the GTO. "Uh, Dad, I think we're going to have to go on to River Dream and get the Cherokee."

My father frowned. "Now that you mention it, I guess that would be a good idea. I don't think the Goat is going to be able to hold everything you're planning to pick up."

That being the case, we drove out to River Dream, pulled the Cherokee out, and parked the GTO. We had lunch at the Minnesott Grill before heading back to New Bern.

Once I'd picked up the supplies I needed in New Bern, we headed straight for Oriental, picking up Highway 55 once we crossed to the east bank of the Neuse. As we passed through the town of Stonewall, my eyes were drawn to the old boat lying half-submerged next to the bridge.

"Dad, how long do you suppose that old boat has been sitting there?"

Sitting forward in his seat so he could see the derelict as we drove over the bridge, my father replied, "I don't know, Michael. It's been there in that run-down boat house for as long as I can remember. It must have been there twenty years."

I slowed down as we drove over the bridge so I could get a good look at the boat.

"I'd say it's been there longer than that. When I was a kid and first saw it, it looked like it had already been sitting there for that long."

"Could be," my father agreed, settling back into his seat.

"I wonder how it got there," I said. "Why do you suppose it was left there to rot?"

It was a wooden boat, looked to be about a twenty-six footer. It was, or had been, a white boat. The deck and cabin roof had been weathered nearly gray, with traces of brown holding out against the elements. All the colors were faded and dirty. The boat listed a bit to its starboard side, the side towards the highway, and the stern on that side had become nearly submerged. The boat was pulled into the boat house bow first, and the way the old structure had collapsed down on it, the bow couldn't be seen from the bridge as we drove past.

The boat house itself was located practically touching the Highway 55 Bridge there in Stonewall. Keeping one eye on the road, I examined it out the driver's side window as we drove past on our way to Oriental.

"It is hard to imagine anyone building a boathouse that close the bridge," I said.

"I wouldn't be surprised to find the remains of an old fishing camp in the woods nearby," my father said.

"That old boat is kind of big to be this far up the creek," I noted. "I wonder if you could even motor back downstream if you managed to refloat it."

My father turned around to look at it as we drove past. "I have a feeling that vessel and the boat house are both permanent parts of the marsh now," he said.

It was hard to imagine someone getting that big of a boat as far up the creek as the boat house was, but someone obviously did. Of course this was as far upstream as they could have gone as the bridge wasn't high enough off the water to allow boat traffic under it.

As it had so many times, the mystery of the boat plagued my mind. "You have to wonder what the story is with that old boat," I continued. "Who owned it first; where did they buy it? I imagine it was someone's pride and joy once upon a time."

"I imagine it was," my father agreed. "It would be interesting to find out who they were and where they are now, to find out why they just left it there for the river to claim. I guess we'll never know."

In Oriental we visited Jeremy at the marina to confirm the new boat would be delivered on time Wednesday. He assured us that everything was on schedule.

Jeremy pulled off his ball cap and wiped a bead of sweat from his forehead with the back of his hand. "Mike, have you thought up a name for her yet?"

This was something Maeve and I had discussed; however, we hadn't agreed on anything. Now I would have to come up with a name myself.

"Actually, Jeremy, I was thinking of calling her *Cuarto*," I said.

Setting his cap back on his head, he gave me a puzzled look. "Kwardo, what does that mean?"

Feeling a tad facetious, I said, "It's Spanish for fourth. She'll be my fourth sailboat."

Jeremy laughed and shook his head. "I get it," he said, "but I don't think that's really Spanish."

I laughed too. "Actually, it really is," I said. "Can we get that name on her sometime before Labor Day?"

"I reckon so. Why before Labor Day?" Jeremy asked.

"Dad and I are setting sail for the Bahamas after Labor Day," I told him.

"That's the date you chose, eh?" Jeremy said. "I'm glad to hear your dad's going with you. Not that I don't think you could handle it, Mike, don't get me wrong. But there's safety in numbers."

"I know what you mean, Jeremy," I said, grateful for his concern.

We left the marina and went to Arapahoe to pick up some groceries at Bellagio's. Grace at the register offered me her condolences. "Your Maeve was a real sweet girl, Michael. She always had a kind word when she came in here."

I shoved my wallet into my pocket and picked up the remaining grocery bags. "Thank you, Grace. Thanks for your kind words," I said.

"Well, now, Michael, you take care now, you hear," Grace said.

"Yes, ma'am, I will," I promised her as I made my way to the door.

Once in the car, I confided to my dad. "I know they all mean well, but each time it's almost like the wound reopens just a little, and it stings."

"Son, I can't say I know what you're going through, but you're right, they mean well. Keep that in mind, and let them say what they feel they need to say. They're going to anyway."

Back at River Dream we fried up a couple of hamburgers and worked on our sailing schedule. My dad would sail with me to Fort Lauderdale and then catch a plane home. From Fort Lauderdale I would sail over to the Bahamas, spend some time among the islands, and then maybe cross back to the

Keys. After that, well, after that would just have to wait and see. I let my friends know that at different points in the voyage they were welcome to come aboard to spend some time.

I also planned several visits home. Thanksgiving, Christmas, Easter, and of course Malori's eighteenth birthday were on the schedule. If Malori hadn't graduated high school a year early, I would have had to include her graduation on that list.

Pushing back from the table, my father said, "Well son, I think we've covered about everything I can think of. We've got the charts we need. Our itinerary seems to cover the contingencies. I guess we're as ready as we can be."

"I think you're right, Dad," I agreed. "It's late, and we have a busy day tomorrow. Let's call it a night."

Wednesday morning, over breakfast at the Minnesott Grill, I discussed with my father the idea of selling *Geddaway*, the twenty-six foot Hunter.

"I really don't need a boat that size," I said. "For day sailing and short trips I've still got *Riverscape*. If I want to go on a real excursion, I'll have the Beneteau. I think I should part with the Hunter."

"That sounds reasonable to me," my father said.

"Maybe I could donate it to Camp Riversail, or maybe the community college," I suggested.

My father nodded as he took a sip of his coffee. "I'm sure either one would appreciate it."

"I'll talk to Mr. Cooper to see if the camp wants it first. If they don't I'll see if Pamlico Community College does," I said.

That decided, we finished breakfast and headed to the marina. We had just walked over to the office building when the truck carrying the Beneteau 331 pulled in.

As my father watched, he said, "Michael, I don't think we'll be going anywhere on that boat today."

When I looked at her, I realized he was right; we would not be sailing her out of there anytime very soon.

"Well then, what should we do?" I asked him.

"When was the last time you went surf fishing?" my father asked me by way of reply.

Thirty

"Honestly, probably not since high school," I admitted.

"Well, then, it's about time you went," my father told me. "Let's head up to Fort Macon and see if they're biting in the inlet."

"Why don't we just fire up my Grady-White and head out to the Sound?" I suggested. "I don't think I even have any surf rods."

"Then it sounds like we've got a perfectly good reason to shop for fishing equipment," my father said.

I realized that my dad really wanted to go surf fishing. Or maybe he just wanted to visit Fort Macon. Either way I relented.

"All right Dad," I said. "Let's go surf fishing, after a stop in Atlantic Beach to pick up some surf rods."

After checking with Jeremy, who told us the boat should be ready to go by the end of the week, we headed first to River Dream to unload the Cherokee, and then to Emerald Isle. My father drove. It was less than two miles from River Dream to the Minnesott Ferry landing as the crow flies, but by road it was closer to six. We got there just in time to watch the ferry pull away from the dock. Rather than sit there and wait for the next one, we decided to have lunch at the Minnesott Grill.

"You two must really like our food," Judy, our favorite waitress, said with a smile as we walked in. "Weren't you just here for breakfast?"

"As a matter of fact we were, and we do," my father said in reply to her question.

"Well, come on in and sit down then," Judy said. Turning to me she asked, "So, you beat up any body lately?"

"No Judy, I'm trying to quit," I told her. "Besides I didn't beat them up. I gave them a stern talking to, remember?"

Judy laughed, and said, "I remember. Now what would y'all like for lunch?"

I had a bacon cheeseburger with fries. My dad had the fried chicken sandwich. I left Judy a tip nearly equal to the cost of the meal.

"You shouldn't do that, you know," my father said. "It makes her other customers look bad in comparison."

"She's a single mom with two kids in high school who she wants to see go to college. I do what I can to help," I said a bit defensively.

"She'll probably be eligible for all kinds of financial aid," my father observed.

"Financial aid doesn't cover everything," I said.

"Haven't you given her name to the Lanier Scholarship Fund?" my father asked. The look I gave him answered for me.

"I should have known," he said.

"You know, Dad," I said, "by the time we get to the beach, buy the tackle, and get to Fort Macon, we won't have a lot of time to fish."

"So?" was all he said. I shrugged and got into the

Cherokee. Dad got behind the wheel, and we headed to the ferry landing. There was a short line, and we could see the ferry approaching the dock. We didn't have to wait long.

Once we were on board the ferry, my father said, "We can fish until dark and then head into Morehead City. You can buy me supper at the Sanitary Fish Market."

"I can buy you supper," I said in mock indignation.

"Hey, I'm doing all the driving," he laughed. I smiled and realized I was glad he was dragging me to the beach. It was time away from more familiar surroundings that would do me some good.

By Friday, *Cuarto* was ready for the water. My father stayed on and sailed with me when the representative from Beneteau took me out for a familiarization day of sailing. By evening, I felt confident I could handle her at least as far as River Dream. The representative left shortly after we returned to the marina. My father and I drove to River Dream, leaving *Cuarto* tied up at the marina dock, and returned to sail her home Saturday morning. Sunday morning my dad drove back to Wrightsville Beach in my GTO. He would take care of storing it while I was gone.

Monday I went over to Camp Riversail and talked with Mr. Cooper about *Geddaway*.

"Michael, I would be glad to accept your Hunter 26. It would be a great addition to the program for the older campers," Mr. Cooper said.

That decided, I worked out the details with Captain Jack, and we drove to the Marina to let Jeremy know. Since the summer camp season had pretty much wound down, we'd decided to let *Geddaway* winter at the marina. Jack would come get her in the spring to get her ready for next summer's season.

Then it was back to River Dream, where I would spend

the next couple of days climbing all over *Cuarto,* getting to know her every nook and cranny.

My father returned on Friday night, this time in his Suburban, and on Saturday we took *Cuarto* out for an overnight trip up to Rockhole Island and back. We anchored overnight in a cove and then sailed back on Sunday without making landfall along the way. It gave us some idea of what living aboard was going to be like.

Sunday evening, just after my dad left to go back to Wrightsville Beach, Rhiannon called.

"Hi, Michael," she said. "How's the new boat? You did pick her up already, right?"

"She's a beauty," I said. "My dad and I took her out this weekend for an overnight sail, and it was great."

"I'm glad. So, will you be leaving soon?" Rhiannon asked.

"We won't leave until after Labor Day," I said.

"We," Rhiannon questioned with an odd inflection. "You're not going alone?"

"My dad's going with me, at least for the first leg. When we get to Lauderdale he's going to fly home, and I'll head to the Islands alone."

"Oh, your dad's going with you," she said with relief in her voice.

"Who did you think was going with me?" I teased.

"I'm just glad you're not heading out alone is all," Rhiannon said, ducking the question.

"No, I'm not," I assured her.

"That's good," she said. "Will you be around next weekend? Let me rephrase; would you and your dad be able to come to Greenville next weekend to help my dad get me moved?"

"I know I can, and I imagine he can," I told her. "I'll call him in a while when he's had a chance to get home. I'll let you know what he says."

"Thanks, Mike," Rhiannon said. "I'll talk to you then."

My father was able to make it. The three of us - me, my dad, and Rhiannon's dad - converged on her apartment Saturday morning. Between Uncle Lind's pickup, my father's Suburban, and the panel truck I rented, we were able to load up all her stuff and make only one trip. Late that Saturday afternoon, we arrived at the Nadeau House and began unloading Rhiannon's stuff. Both our mothers and Malori, were there to help. When we were done, we feasted on pizza delivered from Dupree's.

"I didn't think Alfred delivered out here to the Island." I said.

Malori gave me a scornful look. "He has ever since he opened up a new location out here."

Rhiannon seemed as surprised as I was. "When did that happen?" she asked.

"He opened the new place last spring sometime. Don't tell me you didn't notice," Malori said.

Reaching for another slice, I said, "I guess I didn't. I sure am glad he did, though. This really hits the spot."

I hung around after everyone left to help Rhiannon get settled and make sure she knew where all the switches and shut-offs were. "If there's anything you want to change to make you feel more at home, Rhiannon, please just go ahead and do it. You have free reign to make this place your own."

"I may take you up on that, Mike. Even though I know you lived here for years, it still feels like Mrs. Nadeau's house to me," Rhiannon said. "I still remember French Club meetings right here in this living room. We made French Onion Soup in her kitchen."

Smiling at her nostalgic reminiscence, I reiterated, "Rhiannon, anything you want to change, you can change.

This is your place now."

"It's mine for a while anyway, Mike. Thank you."

Stifling a yawn, I glanced at my watch. "I guess I'd better get going. I've got a long drive home."

Rhiannon seemed about to say something but stopped herself. "Thank you again, Mike, for everything. I'll see you next time you're in town?"

"You can count on it, though I don't know when that will be. I'll write you and let you know how the trip is going."

"You had better," Rhiannon said. "And I intend to hold you to that promised lunch when you're in town."

"I know you will," I said. "In fact, I'm counting on it."

Rhiannon looked at me quizzically for a second. "Bon Voyage, Michael," she said as she hugged me.

When I got to the truck, I turned around to wave good-bye, but she'd already gone inside. I climbed in and began the long drive back to River Dream.

Thirty-one

My dad and I left River Dream aboard a fully provisioned *Cuarto* on the day after Labor Day. We traversed the Inland Waterway to Beaufort and spent the first night tied up at the town docks. Working our way about twenty-five miles a day down the coast, alternating between the ocean, the sounds, and the waterway, we arrived at my mom and dad's house on the evening of the fourth day of our cruise.

Mom and Malori made a big deal out of our arrival. Mom cooked her special chicken supreme for the occasion. Since it was probably the last home-cooked meal we would have for a while, I had two extra helpings.

My father slept in his own bed that night. I slept on the boat. I called Rhiannon, but she wasn't home, so I walked up to the pier and, sure enough, there she was behind the counter.

"Hey sailor, I thought you'd be in Nassau by now," Rhiannon said.

"Not quite yet," I laughed. "Four days at sea and this is as far south as we've gotten."

Rhiannon laughed with me. "Well, you did say you'd be

stopping in on your way by."

"Yeah, but we're heading out at O-Dark-Thirty," I said.

"Then shouldn't you be getting some sleep?" Rhiannon asked, frowning with concern.

"I should, you're right. I just wanted to stop by and say 'Hi' since I was here."

"I'm glad you did, Mike," Rhiannon said.

I stayed for a little while longer. She told me how she was settling in to her new job and the house. I told her what it was like sailing with my dad. All too soon I realized I needed to get back to the boat to get some sleep. I said good-night and left Rhiannon to her work.

Ten days after pulling away from my folk's dock on Masonboro Sound, my father and I were hunkered down in Savannah, Georgia, waiting out Hurricane Hugo. We were very lucky to find a place for *Cuarto* that allowed her to weather the storm with no significant damage. What harm was done was fixed up in a day, and we were back underway.

Savannah wasn't in the direct path of the hurricane. That honor was reserved for Charleston, South Carolina. Once the storm passed and the seas were safe to venture out on, we left Savannah and set sail south. Two weeks later we docked in Fort Lauderdale. My father and I spent a few days in Fort Lauderdale relaxing while he helped me make sure *Cuarto* was ship shape for the crossing to the islands. Then he caught a flight home, and I caught a west wind for the Bahamas.

When Thanksgiving came, I sent home my regrets that I wouldn't be able to make it home for the holiday. A week after Thanksgiving, Hans had joined me on board *Cuarto* to spend a week of vacation sailing the Islands. When he flew home, Hans took with him my gifts for everyone and my explanation of why I was staying in the Islands for Christmas. I just wasn't ready to face the holidays without Maeve. There in the Islands I could pretend, in a manner of speaking, that they weren't really happening.

Chase, who was teaching technology at North Carolina State, joined me for a couple of weeks right after Christmas. We spent New Year's Eve on Saint Croix. I wound up dancing with Rochelle, a beautiful young lady from Rouen, France.

Rochelle's skin was the color of cafe au lait, her hair was long and black, and her eyes were so dark I couldn't tell the irises from the pupils. Her father was from Senegal, and her mother was from Aruba. I never did quite understand how they came to be in Rouen - something about the company Rochelle's father worked for. Rochelle was a second year student at the American University in Paris, on Saint Croix with some school friends for the holiday.

I don't know what attracted Rochelle to me. Maybe it was the grizzled sailor look or the deep tan I'd developed over all those months at sea. It could be that she just liked older guys more than the school boys among her peers.

Why didn't really matter. We enjoyed the evening talking and dancing, but when the party broke up I'm afraid I disappointed her when Rochelle suggested that we could go back to her room. While I'd enjoyed her company, I wasn't looking for anything like that. Rochelle said she understood, thanked me for the evening, kissed me gently, and said good-bye.

"Mike," a noticeably inebriated Chase said. "I don't know how you let her just walk away. She obviously dug you."

As I tried to steer him toward the dock, I wondered that myself. "Yeah, I know. Maybe I'm an idiot, but it just didn't feel like the right thing to do."

Chase nodded his agreement. "Anyway, I guess we need to head back to the boat. You drive."

Being that the club was only a short walk from the harbor, and we had indeed walked there, Chase was acknowledging that perhaps he'd had a bit too much to drink and needed my help finding his way back to the dock. Perhaps if I had taken a drink of something stronger than club soda and lime, I would have followed Rochelle back to her room. I put my arm around Chase's shoulder, and we found our way back to *Cuarto*.

When the season for college spring break approached, I made port and arranged to leave *Cuarto* docked for a week or so while I flew home to spend time with the folks. The sea, sun, wind, and friendly folks on the Islands had been working their therapeutic magic on me. I was feeling much more at peace with myself.

Thirty-two

Malori, who was home for Spring Break, picked me up at the airport in my GTO the Monday afternoon I arrived.

"Dad thought you might like to drive your own car while you're home," she explained.

"That was thoughtful of him," I said, holding my hand out for the keys. "And you just happened to be available to drive it out here to meet me."

"Hey, what can I say, I've missed my big brother," Malori said.

We got into the car. I drove. We headed out to the beach.

"How long are you going to stay home, Mike?" Malori asked once we were on the road.

"I'll be here at least a week, maybe longer. My return ticket is for next Monday. I can always change that if I decide to," I said.

"It hardly seems worth going all that way back just to turn around and come back for Easter," Malori said.

My coming back for Easter wasn't a sure thing, but I didn't want to tell her just then.

D W Davis

"What are you talking about? I'll get in more than two good weeks of cruising," I said instead.

Snickering, Malori said, "The Islands will never be the same."

I laughed. "What are you trying to say, sister mine?"

"Oh, nothing at all," Malori said with all the innocence she could muster. "You know that UNCW is closed all this week."

"It usually is," I said.

Malori looked sideways at me as we rode along Eastwood Road. "That means that Rhiannon is off all this week."

"That would stand to reason," I said.

"You did say you would take her out to lunch when you were home," Malori reminded me.

"I said we could get together for lunch," I corrected her. "That's not quite the same as taking her out."

"You are splitting hairs," Malori said. "I told her you were coming home today."

"You didn't have to do that," I told her as we stopped for the light at the drawbridge. "I had written and told her last time I made landfall near a post office."

"I know," Malori informed me, "she told me."

"Do you and Rhiannon talk much?" I asked, feigning annoyance.

"When I was at UNCW I would see her almost every day. We usually had breakfast together at the Hawks' Nest before she went to work," Malori told me. "Once I went off to Notre Dame, we wrote each other a lot. She kept me up to date on what was going on around here, and I kept her in the loop on what I'd heard from you."

The light turned green, so I put the car in gear and we rolled over the bridge. "Oh, really, isn't that interesting."

192

"We ran into each other a couple of mornings early last semester and it just sort of became a routine," Malori explained. "She's been kind of like a big sister to me."

That brought a twinge. I could see it did for Malori, too. Maeve had been the big sister Malori had longed for. I guess I was glad Rhiannon had been there to step into that role and yet…

Looking at me, Malori said, "I still miss her too, Michael."

"Yeah," was all I managed to say as I fought back tears. We rode the rest of the way to our folks' house lost in our own thoughts.

Thirty-three

My father must have had some kind of early warning radar. He was waiting for us at the bottom of the steps when we pulled down the road to the house. He came around to the driver's side as I shut off the engine.

"Welcome home, Michael. How was your flight?"

"It was long and circuitous," I told him as I climbed from the car. "I couldn't go straight from there to here. I had to go several other places first."

He laughed, "It still beat walking, I reckon."

"Yes, it did. Especially since I would have to swim a lot before I could walk," I joked back.

He gestured to the stairs. "Well, come on inside. Your mom's dying to see you."

When I went into the kitchen, I could smell lasagna baking in the oven.

"Hi, Mom, that smells delicious," I said as I gave her a hug.

"I am glad you think so. I have been keeping it warm for you since your birthday," my mother said with a straight face. "You did not show up to eat it."

"It was a long swim against an outgoing tide," I offered as a way of excuse.

"I am sure it was. It is good to see you, Michael," my mother said.

I closed my eyes and took a deep breath, drawing in the familiar scents of home. "It's good to be here," I said.

"It still has a while to bake, so we can sit down and you can tell me all about your travels," my mother said, wiping her hands on a towel and pulling out a chair.

My father fixed us some iced tea, and we sat around the kitchen table while I told them all about what I'd been up to since I dropped my father off in Fort Lauderdale.

By the time I finished my story, my mother announced that supper was ready. I'd just stood up to see what I could do to help when I heard a car pull up outside.

Looking from me to the door and back at me, my mother said, "I hope you do not mind, Michael; I invited Rhiannon to join us."

Since it must have been Rhiannon who'd just driven up, I don't think it mattered much if I minded or not. My father and Malori went out to meet her.

Presented with a fait accompli, I chose to be gracious. "No, I don't mind. It will be good to see her."

Interestingly enough, as soon as I said it, I realized that it really would be good to see her.

"Rhiannon has been such a good friend to Malori since she moved back. And she has been looking forward to seeing you as well," my mother told me.

"Really," I said, a bit surprised. "Do you see her often?"

"In the evenings your father and I usually take a walk up to the pier. It is how we get our exercise. Rhiannon has been helping Ed and Lind out in the evenings now and then. We usually have a chance to chat while your dad is talking with the guys."

"Is that how you've kept your youthful figure, Mom?" I asked with a grin.

Blushing lightly, my mother laughed, "Michael, do not be fresh. But thank you for noticing."

I got up from the table and went out onto the deck. Rhiannon had just started up the stairs. She looked up, spotted me, and broke into a big smile.

I thought she looked even prettier than she did in high school, and then felt oddly guilty for thinking that.

"Hi, Michael," she called out. "It's about time you came home. Your mom's been keeping a pan of lasagna warm for you since Veteran's Day."

"Did you two work that joke out or what?" I retorted.

"Who's joking?" Rhiannon asked as she reached the top of the stairs. "It's good to see you, Mike," she said, pulling me to her for a big hug.

"It's good to see you too, Rhiannon." I said, and found that I meant it. "I'm glad Mom invited you over."

"Me, too. I love your Mom's lasagna," Rhiannon said with a grin.

"Let's get inside," I said, shaking my head and chuckling.

My dad and Malori came up the stairs after Rhiannon. Dad followed her inside. Malori stopped next to me on the deck.

"I told you she'd be glad to see you," Malori said in a conspiratorial whisper.

"Who woulda thunk it," I replied. "I figured she'd have a boyfriend by now."

"It's not like guys haven't tried, Michael," Malori said. "But Rhiannon wouldn't give them the time of day."

Feeling a sudden need to change the subject, I asked "What about you, Mal?"

Malori answered by sticking her tongue out and dashing into the house. Left alone on the deck for a moment, I looked out over the sound. A stiff breeze was kicking up little whitecaps on the water.

The wind was blowing out of the northwest. That meant a cold night coming on, cold and clear. Shivering just a bit at the thought, I joined the others inside.

My mom put me at the foot of the table opposite my father. That was usually her place. Instead she sat on the corner near my father and next to Rhiannon. Malori sat on the corner near me across from Rhiannon. That put Rhiannon at my other corner.

I thought to myself that there should be some young man of Malori's acquaintance sitting in the empty chair. Once the lasagna had been served and we'd begun eating, I broached that subject again.

"Malori," I began in a teasing tone, "I may regret asking this as it may mean I have to beat someone up, but are you seeing anyone?"

"No one will go out with me," Malori said, laughing. "They're all afraid of you."

"That's good - just as it should be," I said.

"Michael, you're incorrigible. There are lots of nice young men at school that Malori could go out with," Rhiannon said. "It's just that she has very high standards."

"That's right, I do," agreed Malori. "There aren't many guys who can measure up. I mean look at who they're being measured against."

"I think that's a good thing," my father said. "There's no reason to hurry in that department."

"Actually, Michael, your sister does date now and then but has wisely chosen not to start a serious relationship," my mother said.

"I've been too busy with my class load at Notre Dame. Nothing against UNCW, but Notre Dame is one tough school," Malori said.

"So who is it you're measuring these guys against, Malori, that makes it so hard for them to make the grade?" I asked, sounding a bit facetious.

A serious look came over Malori's face as she replied, "You and Dad, Mike, that's who."

That hit me like a ton of bricks. I never imagined that Malori would use me as a yardstick. Maybe our father, but not me. My dad looked a bit uncomfortable. I know I felt a little awkward.

"Thank you, Mal, that means a lot," I said.

It took our father a second longer to find his voice. "Yes, Malori, it means a whole lot."

"It may mean I never get a boyfriend. You guys set the bar so doggone high," Malori said with a smile.

"Just don't lower your sights, Malori. And when the right one does come along, don't let him get away," Rhiannon said, looking at me.

My mother broke the tension by asking if anyone was ready for dessert. She'd baked a maple-caramel cheesecake, her own recipe. As full as I was, I wasn't about to turn that down. Neither did anyone else.

"Boy, I'm stuffed," my father said, after we'd finished dessert. "I think I need to take a walk. Anyone want to join me?"

It sounded like a good idea to me, so I said, "I think I will. I hope there's a jacket around here that will fit me. I'm not used to these temperatures."

"We went up to River Dream and brought down some of your winter clothes and jackets," my mother told me. "They're in Malori's old room. I guess it'll be your room now when you're home."

That surprised me. It used to be my mother's music room. When I walked in, I saw that it still was. They'd put a twin bed along one wall for me. Malori had set my bag on the foot of the bed.

As I came back out to the kitchen, Malori chimed in, "I'd like to go, too."

"Just let me get my jacket from the car, and I'll come too," said Rhiannon, deciding she didn't want to be left out.

My mother, who is more sensible than the rest of us, opted to stay home out of the cold. The rest of us suited up and headed to the beach. It was dark with a new moon, but it was clear and cold.

Thirty-four

On the beach, we turned north and headed towards Crystal Pier. As we passed the Angevine's house, my father suggested we pay a visit to Rhiannon's folks.

Mrs. Angevine answered the door and smiled when she saw me. "Well, look who's here. Michael, how are you?"

Giving her a quick hug, I replied, "I'm well, Aunt Cassie. How are you?"

"Come on in, all of you. Goodness, what are you doing out on a cold night like this?" Mrs. Angevine asked as she ushered us into the house.

"We filled up so much on Mrs. L's lasagna," Rhiannon explained, "we decided to go for a walk. Is Dad working tonight?"

Mrs. Angevine nodded her head. "Every night these days he's working. He says there isn't enough business to pay someone to mind the pier, so he and your uncle take turns."

I looked at Rhiannon. "Maybe tomorrow night we can give the two of them a night off; what do you say?"

"Are you serious, Michael?" Rhiannon asked, eyes wide with surprise.

"Sure," I said. "Why not? It would be fun. It's not like we haven't minded the store over there before."

"No, but it's been a while, for you anyway," Rhiannon responded. For a minute I didn't think she was going to go along. Then a smile crossed her face and she said, "If you really want to, let's do it."

Mrs. Angevine looked pleased at the prospect. "That would be so nice, you two. I know your daddy will appreciate it, Rhiannon."

That decided, we bid Rhiannon's mother good-bye and headed back towards Lumina Pier. We told Mrs. Angevine we would stop by and let Mr. Angevine know.

Mr. Angevine was more surprised than Rhiannon had been at the suggestion. "You two would do that? But Michael, it's your holiday," he argued.

"I feel like I've been on holiday since summer, Uncle Lind. Doing some honest work will do me some good."

Putting his arms around the two of us, he said, "Well, I certainly won't turn down your offer. I'm sure my brother will be glad of it, too."

While my father stayed back to talk to Mr. Angevine, Rhiannon, Malori, and I took a walk out onto the pier. The wind was cold and bit right through our coats.

I shouldn't have been, but I was surprised to see Hans' mom fishing. "Mrs. Schultz, what a pleasant surprise."

Putting down her rod, she walked over and gave me a hug. "Michael, is that you? I heard you were off pretending to be a Caribbean pirate."

"The Royal Navy was on to me, so I decided to come home and lay low for a while," I said, going along with the joke.

Holding me at arms' length, she looked me up and down. "Well, it's good to see you. Have you been doing okay?"

"I've been doing a little better every day, Mrs. Schultz, thank you."

She nodded as she considered that. "Hans is looking forward to rejoining your crew next month. I think it will do him a world of good."

"It will be great to have him along," I said. "I need someone to swab the deck and mizzen the jib once in a while." Behind me, Rhiannon and Malori laughed.

"I'm sure you two young men will enjoy yourselves out there with all those Island ladies to keep your minds off your troubles," Mrs. Shultz commented.

Hans and April had separated just after New Year's Day. I suppose it was what you would call an amicable divorce. She got the kids, and he got the bills. Hans had told me he thought sailing around the Caribbean with me for a couple of weeks would be just what he needed to take his mind off it.

"I'll try to be a bad influence on him, Mrs. Schultz," I promised lightheartedly.

"You do that, Michael," she said. "It may be just what he needs."

Leaving her to her fishing, we walked on to the end of the pier. The wind felt stronger out there, and no fisherman were bold enough to challenge it that night. I looked up and scanned the clear skies, almost unconsciously picking out Star Jillian. I smiled a melancholy smile at that memory.

"What was that smile, son?" my father asked.

I hadn't realized he'd come out onto the pier. He and I were out there alone. Rhiannon and Malori had headed back inside. I'd been stargazing longer than I realized.

"I was just remembering something from a long time ago, Dad," I said. "Do you remember Jill? She and I dated for a while in high school before Rhiannon and I got together."

My father pursed his lips and I could tell he was stretching his memory. "Yes, Michael, I remember Jill. She was that pretty blond girl who swept you off your feet when you first started at Laney. What made you think of her?"

I pointed to the stars. "See that faint star there, about forty degrees above the horizon? That's the star I bought for her. That's Star Jillian."

Laughter shook my father's shoulders. "I'd forgotten all about you buying Jill a star for Valentine's that year," he said. "Whatever happened to her?"

"The last I heard she was living in Asheville with that artist fella she married," I said. "I haven't spoken to her since high school."

A cold gust reminded me I wasn't in the Caribbean anymore. "Let's follow the girls inside before we freeze," I suggested.

Bidding Mrs. Schultz good fishing as we went by, we returned to the pier house. Malori and Rhiannon had taken seats at one of the tables and were sipping hot chocolate. Uncle Lind brought my father and me some fresh coffee. To my surprise there was a dollop of maple syrup flavoring it.

"Your dad comes for coffee just about every morning now after his walk," explained Mr. Angevine, "so I started keeping a bottle of the syrup in the cooler for him."

Turning a concerned eye on my father, I asked, "Are you walking every morning too, Dad?"

My father made a dismissive gesture. "My doctor said it would be good for my heart. Your mother rather insisted that I begin a routine. She walks with me in the evening."

"Is there something wrong with your heart?" I asked, worried.

"No, no, there's nothing wrong yet. The walking is a preventative measure," my father assured me.

Malori finished her hot chocolate. "We should probably be getting home," she suggested. "Mom's probably starting to wonder if we washed out with the tide."

"I think we can finish our coffee," my father said. "Then we'll go."

Something about the look on Rhiannon's face caused me to say, "If you don't think Mom will be upset, I'd like to stay for a second cup."

Rhiannon smiled and said, "I could use another hot chocolate, too."

My father smiled a knowing smile. "Your mother is a very understanding woman, Michael. I'm sure she won't mind."

"Then I'll stay too," Malori said, starting to sit back down.

"Mal, you better see that Dad makes it home okay," I suggested to her.

"Oh, I can do that," Malori said with a smirk.

"Thanks, sis, you're my best sister," I said. Malori hugged me before she left with our father.

Rhiannon was giving me a funny look. "You are full of odd things to say tonight, Michael. You need Hans to mizzen the jib. Malori is your best sister. Does that make me your best friend?"

I couldn't help but laugh. "Watch out or I'll mizzen your jib. When I was leaving home to join the Navy, Malori told me I was her best brother. She was only seven at the time. Since then it's been kind of our code for saying 'I love you' without being all mushy about it."

A warm smile replaced the funny look on Rhiannon's face. "That is very sweet, Michael. It's your fault, you know."

Wondering what I'd done now, I asked, "What's my fault?"

"It's your fault that Malori can't find a steady boyfriend," Rhiannon informed me. "She compares the guys she dates to her big brother, and they always come up short."

Looking down into my coffee cup, I demurred, "I'm not that much to compare to."

"To Malori you are," Rhiannon said. "And someday she'll find the guy that measures up, and she'll be glad she waited."

We finished our drinks and walked back to my folks' house. I almost reached out to take her hand - almost.

When we got to her car, Rhiannon asked me to say good-night and thanks to my folks for her. She gave me a hug, got in her car, and left. I went into the house. My mom and dad had already gone to bed, but Malori was up watching television.

Looking up from whatever show it was she was watching, she asked, "Did you and Rhiannon have a nice talk?"

Taking a seat in one of the recliners, I answered, "Yes, we did."

"What did you talk about?" Malori asked.

"You, mostly," I said.

Turning around so that she faced me, Malori exclaimed, "Me! What did you talk about me for?"

Not able to resist teasing her a little, I said, "You are a very interesting subject. I've been thinking about taking some psychology classes just so I can figure you out."

She stuck her tongue out at me. "Fery vunny, Mike," she said.

"I haven't heard that in a while," I said, feeling a nostalgic twinge.

"I picked it up from Rhiannon," Malori said.

"I figured," I told her. Realizing I was exhausted, I decided to go to bed. "Good-night, Mal."

"Good night, Michael. I'm glad you're home."

Thirty-five

When I woke up in my mother's music room the next morning, it took me a moment to remember where I was. I hadn't slept that well, both because of all the coffee I had at the pier and because I wasn't used to sleeping on solid land.

Pulling on some sweats, I headed out to the deck for my morning workout. As I finished up, my dad came out on the deck dressed for his morning walk.

"Do you mind if I join you?" I asked.

"I don't mind at all," he said. "I'll be glad for the company."

He did a few stretching exercises and commented on how he could see his breath in the cold air. The wind had changed overnight, and some clouds had moved in, but it was still brisk.

"Did you and Rhiannon have a nice visit last night after Malori and I left?"

"Yes, we did," I said. "We talked about Malori."

"Really," my father said, sounding surprised. "What about Malori?"

I filled him in on what Rhiannon told me. "We talked

about how she can't find a boyfriend who measures up to the high standards we've set for male behavior. According to Rhiannon, we have ruined that girl for most men with our high level of morality and trustworthiness."

"It must be all that time we spent in Boy Scouts," my father quipped.

"It must be," I agreed.

Done with his stretching, my father headed for the steps. "As her dad, I rather like it that she hasn't had a serious boyfriend."

"As her dad, you'd probably be happier if she decided to become a nun," I joked as I followed him to the road.

My father shook his head. "No, not really, though she is going to Notre Dame, so maybe there's hope."

I'd been wondering how that was going for her. "How's she done up there? Has the change been good for her?"

"I think it has. She didn't decide it on the spur of the moment. She researched it and thought about it for quite some time," my father reminded me.

"I thought she kept it a big secret," I said.

"She thought she did too. Parents know things, son," my father said, giving me one of those looks.

"I won't ask what sort of things you knew about me," I said.

"It's probably best you don't," my father said with such a serious expression that for a moment I was worried.

"Hey, I never did anything that bad," I protested.

"No, I guess you didn't," my father admitted with a smile. He'd gotten me good. We neared the end of his walk. He did about two miles up and down the beach each morning. It always finished up at the pier where he would get his daily cup of coffee.

Rhiannon's uncle was at the counter. If I understood

Aunt Cassie correctly, they traded twelve-hour shifts this time of year when business was slow. That's quite a grind when you're open twenty-four hours a day seven days a week.

"Good morning Mr. Angevine," I said as we walked up to the counter.

Rhiannon's uncle stepped out from behind the counter to greet us, "Michael, good morning. Good morning, Owen."

"Good morning, Ed," my father said, taking a seat on a stool at the counter. Rhiannon's uncle's name was Edmond.

"Michael, what's with the Mr. Angevine? It's Ed," he said, sounding disappointed I'd been so formal.

"I'm sorry, Ed. I guess it's just been a while," I apologized.

"It's not a problem. Owen, coffee?" Ed asked, going behind the counter and picking up the pot.

"Yes, please," my father said.

"Mike?" Ed asked, gesturing with the coffee pot in my direction.

"The same, please," I said as I sat down beside my dad.

"Do you like yours the way your dad takes his?" Ed asked.

Realizing he meant did I take mine with maple syrup, I replied, "Yes, please."

"Coming right up," Ed said. "Mike, Lind told me that you and Rhiannon are going to spell us today. He said he didn't know what time, though."

"Truthfully, I don't think we thought about that, Ed," I said. "What would be a good time?"

Setting our cups down on the counter, Ed said, "We usually go twelve to twelve. If you and my niece were to come on at six tonight and work through to six in the morning, Lind could get to spend some time with the Missus, and I could get a good night's sleep."

The way he said the last remark made me think it had been a while since he'd had a good night's sleep.

"I'll call Rhiannon and let her know," I said.

We finished our coffee and headed to the house where my mother had prepared us a hearty breakfast of bacon and scrambled eggs. Malori was gone to the aquarium by the time we got back. She'd told me that so many of the volunteers from the college were away for Spring Break that the volunteer coordinator had practically begged Malori to work extra shifts.

I spent the rest of the morning with my father, going over business stuff. He insisted it would be a good idea if I had at least some understanding of just what was going on with all those investments. I was glad when lunch time finally arrived as I was picking Rhiannon up for lunch.

We were going to Dupree's. It had been a long time since I'd eaten a good Dupree's pizza, not since the day we helped Rhiannon move from Greenville. I decided I wasn't waiting any longer.

"Well, well, well, if it isn't my old friend Michael," Alfredo said as Rhiannon and I walked in.

Smiling at his boisterous greeting, I embraced my friend. "Hello, Alfredo," I said. "How have you been? How's business?"

Slapping me on the back, Alfredo assured me, "Business has been good, Michael, and I have been good, too."

He ushered us to a table. His restaurant on the island was quite different from his place in town. The atmosphere was much brighter, and there were plenty of windows.

"Rhiannon," Alfredo said to her, "what are you doing hanging around with this character?"

"In a weak moment I agreed to let him buy me lunch, Alfredo," Rhiannon said smiling. "Then I couldn't find a good excuse to get out of it."

Alfredo laughed and said, "Well I, for one, like seeing the two of you together. It reminds me of when you were kids."

He left on that note and sent a waitress right over to our table.

Taking out her order pad she said, "The boss said to take good care of you guys, that you're old friends of his."

"We've known Alfredo a long time," I told her.

"That's cool," she said, sounding impressed. "My name is Bella, short for Isabella, and I'll be taking care of you. What can I bring you to drink?"

"I'd like some sweet tea," Rhiannon said.

"The same for me," I told her.

Jotting down our drink order, she said, "Two sweet teas coming up. Are you ready to order some food?"

I looked at Rhiannon and she shrugged to indicate that she would eat whatever I ordered.

"What I'd like is a large pizza with pepperoni, peppers, and onions," I told Bella.

"All right, anything else?" Bella asked.

Before I could add anything, Rhiannon said, "I think that will be plenty. After all, I have to watch my figure."

"I'm sure we can find plenty of volunteers to watch your figure for you, Rhiannon," I quipped.

"Brat," Rhiannon retorted. Bella laughed and went off to place our order.

The pizza was as delicious as I'd been anticipating and, despite Rhiannon's doubts, we, mostly me, managed to finish off the whole thing. I was stuffed and figured it would take a couple of miles up and down the beach to work off our lunch, but I didn't care. It had been months since I'd had a Dupree's pizza, and I enjoyed every bite.

After lunch we drove down to the aquarium at Fort Fisher to see Malori at work. My father had dug out my membership card and given it to me that morning. It was a Founder's Membership card. Those cards were reserved for patrons who made donations of at least six digits.

Rhiannon knew about the Lanier Marine Science Foundation and that through it my family was a founding member of all three North Carolina Aquariums. I didn't know if the person responsible for hiring Malori knew it or not. I supposed it had probably come up sometime during the application process.

Not that Malori needed the money. I'd set her up with a trust fund that would provide for her for life should she need it. Our mother and father had raised her the same way they did me, though. She would rather earn her way than have it paid for her. In most ways she was better about that than I was.

When the young lady - her name was Lydia according to the name tag pinned just above the North Carolina Aquarium logo on her aquamarine golf shirt - working at the aquarium's ticket window looked at my membership card, her lips curled into a puzzled smile. I realized she'd probably never seen a card like it.

"Sir, could you wait just a moment?" Lydia asked. "I'll be right back."

Thirty-six

I shrugged, smiled, and said, "All right, I'll wait right here."

Lydia went out the door at the back of the ticket booth and over to the information desk.

Rhiannon nudged me and said, "What's the matter? Has your membership expired?"

Before I could reply that my membership never expired, Lydia returned with an older lady wearing a similar aquamarine golf shirt. To my surprise, the older lady was Mrs. Watson, my high school biology teacher.

"Mrs. Watson, is that you?" I asked as she walked up to us.

Not recognizing us right away, she replied, "I am Mrs. Watson, yes."

Then, as recognition set in, she exclaimed, "Michael Lanier, Rhiannon Angevine, well, well, fancy seeing the two of you here, together. It's all right to let them in, dear," Mrs. Watson said Lydia. "Michael and his family are founding members of the aquarium."

Rhiannon and I went inside, and Mrs. Watson met us in

the lobby.

"Michael, I was so sorry to hear about Maeve. She was a dear friend and a fine teacher. We really miss her at Laney."

"Thank you, Mrs. Watson," I said.

She hadn't meant to hurt me. Rhiannon saw the look that started to come over me and gently squeezed me hand.

"It means a lot when I hear she's remembered fondly by her friends and colleagues," I was able to say.

"Yes, yes, well, what can I do for you today?" Mrs. Watson asked, becoming very businesslike.

"I'm back in town for a few days, and thought I'd come see what's new here at the aquarium," I said. "I haven't been here in some time."

"Well, I know just the person to give you your tour. Let me see if she's available," Mrs. Watson said.

I thought for a minute that she might be calling Malori to come and act as our tour guide, but I was wrong. At first, I didn't recognize the young lady that came forward. When I saw the name tag 'Emily' I realized it was Beth Bosworth's little sister, only she wasn't so little anymore. I'd heard she'd graduated from the marine science program at Duke about the time I finished up my degree at UNCW.

"Hello Michael, Rhiannon. How are you today?" Emily asked.

"Hi Emily, it has been a long time," Rhiannon said. "How's Beth?"

"She's doing very well. She and Eric just had their second child, a little boy," Emily said.

Beth had married Eric Simpson, a guy she met at East Carolina. When Emily mentioned their new baby, I remembered, vaguely, that Beth had been pregnant at Maeve's funeral. Her oldest was a girl named Michelle. Eric coached football and taught physical education at a high school out near Winston-Salem. Beth was the band director at a middle school in the same district.

"Yes, I got an announcement in the mail," Rhiannon said. Turning to me, she said, "They named him Eric Michael Simpson."

"Really, so he'll be a junior," I said. "That's great."

"Not exactly," Rhiannon said, "Eric's middle name is Lawrence."

She let me hang for a minute before laughing and saying, "Eric's father's name was Michael."

"Fery vunny, Rhiannon," I said.

Emily gave us a confused smile. "Would you like me to show you what's new at the aquarium?"

Giving Rhiannon a scathing look, I said to Emily, "I would like that very much, thank you. We can leave the jolly joker to wait here."

"Oh, no you don't. I didn't come all this way to sit in the lobby," Rhiannon said, still chuckling.

Emily gave us another funny look and started to lead the way into the aquarium. Then she turned around suddenly.

"Malori Lanier works here. Isn't that your sister, Michael?" Emily asked.

Trying to be patient, I admitted, "Yes, she is."

"Would you rather she gave you the tour?" Emily asked. She looked almost afraid that I would say yes.

Truthfully, I assured her, "Actually, no, I'd rather you did."

"Oh," she said with a very pretty smile, "Okay then, we'll start over this way."

Emily had gotten a couple of steps ahead when Rhiannon put her head close to mine and whispered, "Michael J. Lanier, here with me and flirting with her. You have no shame."

Then she stifled a laugh at the look I gave her.

Emily did give us an excellent tour of the place, even taking us behind the scenes to show us areas of the aquarium that are off limits to most guests. During the tour we learned she was close to finishing her master's degree at UNCW.

"If my thesis gets approved, I'll have my Master's by May, Emily told us. "I'm in line for the Assistant Director's job here at the aquarium, but it all depends on my finishing my degree."

We had somehow avoided running into Malori during the tour. I found out when Malori got home that night she'd been out in the marsh collecting specimens. On a cold overcast day like that one turned out to be, collecting specimens in a marsh was not a job I'd have wanted to be doing.

Thanking Emily and Mrs. Watson, Rhiannon and I left the aquarium and headed back to Wrightsville Beach. We both wanted to change and maybe grab a nap before taking over at the pier. When we got to the Nadeau house, I got out of the car and started to go inside with Rhiannon.

She gave me a puzzled look. "Michael, are you going to come in?"

Suddenly it dawned on me, I didn't live there anymore.

"Old habits die hard," I said. "I'll see you at the pier."

I turned to get back in the car.

"Michael, you can come in if you want," Rhiannon said softly.

Part of me wanted to, but I wasn't ready, not quite yet.

Opening the car door, I said, "Another time, Rhiannon, okay?"

"Another time, Michael, when you're ready," she said.

The gentle look on her face almost made me change my mind. Mentally taking a deep breath, I got into the car and drove to my folks'. On the way there, it started to rain.

Thirty-seven

The rain became a steady light sprinkle, the kind of rain that accompanies a warm front. The forecasters said it would probably keep coming down all night and into the next day sometime.

Taking into account the weather, I expected it would be a slow night at the pier. Putting on a foul weather jacket over a sweatshirt and a pair of jeans, I added a pair of allegedly waterproofed leather boots and headed over to the pier.

It was a short walk from my folks' house to Lumina Pier, so I only got a little soaked. Reaching the door of the pier house, I heard a car pulling into the nearly empty parking lot. It was Rhiannon. I waited for her just inside the door.

"Hi, Mike. What a night," she said by way of a greeting.

Shedding my jacket, I said, "I know it. I don't think we'll be very busy tonight."

Rhiannon nodded her agreement. "Only the most diehard fisherman will come out on a night like this."

"Personally, I'm against fishing in the rain," I said, and then glanced at Rhiannon.

"Okay, Hank Jr.," Rhiannon said with a grin. "Let's get

checked in so Dad can start his night off."

We hung up our rain gear and went in to tell Uncle Lind that his relief had arrived.

"Some night you picked to give me a night off," he said. "Believe it or not, there are a couple of guys out there fishing."

Helping myself to a cup of hot coffee, I said, "I believe it. I'm surprised that Mrs. Schultz isn't out there."

"She'll come when it's cold, but she doesn't usually fish in the rain," Uncle Lind said.

"Well, Daddy, you can go on home to Momma," Rhiannon told him. "Mike and I can hold down the fort."

After showing us where everything was and making sure we knew how to operate the new cash register, Uncle Lind finally left. I made up some fresh coffee and, while Rhiannon straightened up the shelves behind the counter, I swept the floor.

About seven one fellow came in, asked how the fish were biting, walked out on the pier, and left. Around eight the rain started coming down harder, and one of the two guys that were out on the pier fishing packed it in.

"I was getting just enough bites to keep me at it when the rain wasn't so bad, but not good enough to put up with this," he told us.

He decided to have a cup of coffee and a piece of crumb cake before he went home. I think he was hoping the rain would let up. It didn't, and after he finished his coffee and cake, he left.

"One diehard left," I noted. "Maybe I should walk out and see how he's doing."

"That might be a good idea," Rhiannon agreed.

I walked down the pier to where the guy was set up, almost all the way to the end. He was sitting there bundled up against the rain, sipping on what by then must have been a very cold cup of coffee, and watching his lines.

"Good evening, sir. How are they biting?" I asked when I got close enough.

"Better than you might think on a night like this, Mike," he said.

I knew the voice but couldn't place it right off. Then he turned towards me with a big grin on his face.

"Wes, you son of a gun, what are you doing out here in this mess?" I exclaimed.

"Mike, I'm home on leave, and tonight's the only night I'll have to go fishing. I promised myself I was going fishing at Lumina Pier tonight, no matter what," Wes said.

I smiled at his determination. "Home on leave. Then you're still in the Corps?"

Wes nodded and said, "Yeah, man, still in. I just made Gunny."

That, as I well knew, was a big deal for a Marine.

"Congrats, man," I said shaking his hand. "It's good to see you." Remembering the day I heard about Wes getting hurt in Beirut, I realized how really glad I was to see him.

"Yeah, you too man. Hey, Mike, I was sorry to hear about Maeve." Wes said. "That really sucked."

"Thanks, Wes. Yeah, it did," I said.

Somehow it didn't sting as much hearing it from Wesley. I don't know why not. Maybe it was because we'd been through so much of the same stuff.

"I'm sorry, man, maybe I shouldn't have brought it up," Wes said.

"No, it's all right. I'm handling it a lot better nowadays," I told him.

We stood quiet in the rain for a few minutes before Wes asked, "What are you up to these days?"

Glad for the change of subject, I brought him up to date. "I've been sailing around the Caribbean for the past several months. I came home for Spring Break. Figured I'd leave the Islands to the college kids. I just got into town yesterday."

"Will you be in town long?" Wes asked.

"I'm leaving next Monday," I said.

Wes frowned. "Awe, man, that's too bad."

I turned my collar up against the cold, wet breeze. "Why's that too bad?"

"I'm home for thirty days, and I'm getting married a week from Saturday. It would have been nice to have you there," Wes said.

Wondering if I might know the bride-to-be, I asked, "Who's the lucky girl?"

"You wouldn't know her," Wes said. He was quiet a moment while he tightened his line with a few cranks of his reel. "I met her in Jacksonville. She's a nice girl. Her family has lived in Onslow County for generations. They weren't too crazy about her dating a Marine, but after they got to know me, they warmed up to the idea."

I congratulated him again and was about to head back in when he asked, "So what are you doing out here on a night like this, Mike? You don't even have your fishing pole."

"I'm working, that's what," I said, chuckling. "Rhiannon and I decided to give her dad and uncle a night off and took the six to six shift for them."

"Is Rhiannon back in town?" Wes asked. "Say, are you two…"

Shaking my head, I said, "No, it's not like that."

Wes bit his lip and looked out over the dark ocean waves. "No, it wouldn't be. Too soon, huh? I understand."

"All right, Wes," I said, getting the feeling it was time to leave him alone. "It's been great talking to you, but I think I'll let you stay out here and fish in the rain if you want to. I'm going back inside and get warm."

Looking at his dripping fishing pole, Wes said, "I can't say as I blame you. I probably won't be far behind."

Back inside I shook out my raincoat and poured myself a fresh cup of coffee, adding a dollop of maple syrup from the cooler.

Rhiannon stopped rearranging the snacks on the display rack long enough to ask, "What in the world kept you out there so long?"

Taking a big sip of the hot coffee, I told her, "I ran into an old friend."

"Really, who is that out there?" she asked, leaning back against the counter.

"Wesley Hunter," I said. "He's home on leave and bound and determined to get in some pier fishing tonight if it kills him."

Rhiannon thought about that for a moment. "Is he still in the Marine Corps?"

"Yup," I replied, taking another sip of coffee. I could feel it starting to chase away the chill.

Coming over to sit next to me at the counter, she asked, "Is he stationed at Camp Lejeune?"

I shook my head. "I don't think so. He said he'd come home on leave to get married. He's marrying a girl from Onslow County. I got the impression he's been away."

"Maybe so," Rhiannon conceded.

Wesley came in about ten, soaked to the skin and chilled to the bone, but with a cooler full of fish. We offered him a cup of coffee, but he said he'd rather just go home and climb into a nice, hot shower.

For the next couple of hours it was just the two of us. We straightened and cleaned and swept until there was nothing left to straighten, clean, or sweep. It rained even harder.

Around midnight a couple of guys came in with their gear and bought passes. They said they had just gotten off work and were bound and determined to get in an hour or so of fishing. It was a tradition with them. They went fishing every Tuesday night after work and weren't going to let a little rain stop them. They bought a half-pound of shrimp, a cup of squid, and two cups of coffee. They joked and said it just didn't seem like a beer night.

The rain finally started to ease up about two in the morning, just about the time the two diehards packed it up and left. I guess it was worth it to them. They caught a mess of fish. By four, the rain had stopped altogether. I went out and walked the length of the pier. A warm wind was blowing, warm being a relative thing. It was warmer than it had been all the day before.

At five, a couple of the early morning regulars came in. They were retired fellows that came and fished every day. They'd been coming for years and had annual passes.

"Well, young lady, it's been a while since I've seen you behind that counter," one of the men said.

Treating him to a warm smile, Rhiannon agreed. "It has been a while, hasn't it, Mr. Proux? What can I get for you this morning?"

"If the griddle is hot, you can fry me a couple of eggs and some country ham. A cup of coffee would go nice with that," Mr. Proux said before taking a seat at one of the tables.

"And how about you, Mr. Davies?" Rhiannon asked the other man.

"I'd just like a plain biscuit and a cup of coffee, thank you kindly," Mr. Davies said as he joined Mr. Proux.

"When did you come back to work for your daddy,

Rhiannon?" Mr. Proux asked when she brought them their coffee.

"I sometimes fill in for him in the evenings. This overnighter was just for this one night, I imagine, sir. My friend Mike is back in town, and we used to work here together when we were in high school. We decided to team up again and give Daddy and Uncle Ed the night off."

"Well that was right nice of you young folks to do that for your daddy," Mr. Proux said. "Wasn't that nice of them, Earl?"

"Right nice of them," Mr. Davies said. Looking hard at me he asked, "Aren't you Owen Lanier's boy?"

"Yes, sir, that's me," I answered, respectfully.

"I've known your dad a good long while, son. He helped me get my business on its feet some years back. He's a good man, your daddy," Mr. Davies said.

"Thank you, sir," I said.

Rhiannon was looking at me inquisitively. I decided no good would come of educating Mr. Davies that the money to help his business was actually mine, not my father's. It didn't bother me at all. I felt pretty proud of my dad.

The two men finished their breakfast and moved out onto the pier. Rhiannon was still busy at the grill.

"Come and get it, Mike, omelet to order. You like ham and cheese right?" she said, putting a plate loaded with the omelet and hash browns up on the counter.

My mouth watered as I eyed the food. "Rhiannon, thank you, you didn't have to do that."

"Enjoy it. It's all the pay you're going to get," Rhiannon informed me.

I laughed and sat down as she put down a similarly loaded plate for herself.

"I suspect we're going to see an influx of the early

morning regulars about the time Uncle Ed is supposed to relieve us," Rhiannon said. "I figure I'll stick around and run the grill for him. You can go ahead and take off once he gets here."

Swallowing a forkful of omelet, I told her, "You aren't getting rid of me that easily. You run the grill, and I'll run the register. That'll give Uncle Ed time to do whatever sort of boss things he has to do when he comes in."

Rhiannon cast me a doubtful grin. "You sure you don't mind?"

"Mind," I said, "I was thinking we ought to do this again tonight."

She straightened up and looked at me closely. "I'd like that, Michael, if you're serious."

"I've got nothing else planned, honey," I said.

Thirty-eight

We both stopped cold. Rhiannon looked at me with a shy smile. I took a deep breath. I waited. I don't know what I was waiting for. Was I waiting for Maeve's memory to accuse me, her ghost to castigate me? I don't know, but nothing happened. I smiled back at Rhiannon. Before either of us could say anything, my father walked in for his morning coffee.

"Well, you two, how did it go?" my father asked. "Did you have any fisherman brave the rain?"

"There weren't many, Dad," I said as I handed him his coffee. "My friend Wes was out there."

Gingerly taking his first sip, my father asked, "Wesley Hunter, from high school; is he still in the Marines?"

"He is. He just made Gunnery Sergeant," I said.

Rhiannon added, "We also had the Tuesday night regulars show up after they got off shift. I think they would come out in anything short of a hurricane."

"I imagine you two are looking forward to heading to the house to get some sleep," my father said.

"Since we've decided to work again tonight, I think that

would be a good idea," I remarked.

"What have you decided to do again tonight?" Ed said as he walked in.

Rhiannon told him. "Mike and I had so much fun last night, Uncle Ed, we've decided to give you and Daddy another night off."

"You kids don't have to do that," Ed protested.

"I know we don't, Ed, but we'd like to if you'll let us," I said.

He confirmed what the look on his face had already told us. "I'm all for it. Rhiannon, I imagine your dad will go along, too."

Rhiannon's dad did go along, and the next night we worked the overnight shift at the pier again. It was a much busier night as the weather was nice and the air blown in on the warm front lingered. During lulls we talked about my sailing odyssey, her new job, and what was going to happen when I finally returned home.

"I think I'll move back here," I said. "I don't think I'll ever feel right at River Dream again."

"But Michael, that place means so much to you," Rhiannon said.

"It did, but now it's too full of memories. I read a book once that recommended that when a place becomes too chocked with memories it is time to leave it and cherish it from afar," I said. "That's how I feel about River Dream."

"What will you do with it if you move back here?" she asked.

"I don't know. I'll probably donate it to the conservancy. Maybe turn the house into a research office for studying the river. Who knows?" I said.

"What will you do here if you come back?" Rhiannon asked guardedly.

I hadn't really thought that far ahead. "Maybe I'll work on my doctorate. Maybe I'll just volunteer down at the aquarium."

Looking around the pier house, I realized we were sitting at the table where we'd spent many evenings doing homework. The old pinball machine we'd been playing when I asked Rhiannon to the Ninth Grade Social still stood in the corner. It felt very much like home.

"Maybe I'll just come here to the pier everyday and go fishing."

Laughing, Rhiannon said, "I can just see you as one of the regulars."

"Hey, I used to come here pretty regularly, didn't I?" I asked.

"I always thought that was so you could see me, not to fish," Rhiannon said with a smile.

"It was," I said softly, smiling back.

When things slowed way down in the wee hours of Thursday morning, Rhiannon broached a subject I know was hard for her to bring up. "Mike, I may be a fool to ask this, but what's going to happen to us?"

I didn't answer right away. I looked down into my coffee cup and carefully considered what to say to her. She waited patiently for my reaction.

Finally, I looked up and met her eyes. I think it was the look in her eyes that made up my mind. In her eyes I saw the old Rhiannon that I saw on the beach the night she begged me not to hate her. In those eyes I saw my friend Rhiannon who was sorry for the hurt she'd caused me and who wanted to find some way, any way, to make it better. In her beautiful green eyes I saw fear and hope, fear that I would reject her overture, and hope that though things could never be like they were back in the day, maybe we could find something in tomorrow for the two of us. Most of all I saw in those eyes the love she had for me.

That may have been a lot to read into that question and that look, but I had known Rhiannon all my life. I thought about Maeve and what she would think. I remembered the promise Maeve had begged me to make with her last breaths.

I had been in love with Rhiannon once. That love had grown cold and been replaced by my love for Maeve. But my Maeve was gone. I felt a hot tear escape my eye and grow cold as it rolled down my cheek.

Maeve was gone, but Rhiannon was here, and the feelings I once had seemed to be coming alive again. Could I fall in love with Rhiannon again? Had I already started to? Looking into her eyes that early spring morning, I knew the answer was yes.

"I think," I said to her as I took her hands in mine, "that we should go sailing."

Epilogue

Rhiannon and I left the pier that morning as soon as her uncle arrived to relieve us. We didn't really talk about it; we just walked to her car and drove to the Nadeau House, her house now. As we pulled into the driveway, Rhiannon hit the button to open the garage door. I felt just a momentary twinge as I looked into the empty garage, but it passed quickly.

Closing the garage door behind us, we got out of the car and walked up the steps into the house. I took a deep breath as we entered the kitchen, but if Rhiannon noticed, she never said anything. We didn't stop at the kitchen. I took her hand, and, with what can only be described as a shy smile, she let me lead her to the master bedroom.

Thank goodness she had completely changed it. It looked nothing like the room Maeve and I had shared. Stopping next to the bed, I turned to her and started to speak, but she put a finger to my lips. Then, very softly, she reached up and pulled my head down to hers and kissed me long and deep. Without a word we undressed, climbed into her bed, and made slow, sweet love. Afterward I held her close as we drifted off to sleep.

Sometime later I woke up to the sounds of pots and pans clanking together. I started to look for my jeans and shirt when I noticed a set of clean clothes - my clothes - on her dresser. They were not the clothes I had on when we came from the pier.

I shrugged my shoulders and put them on. I was glad I'd gotten dressed when I entered the kitchen and found my sister Malori there with Rhiannon.

"Hi, Squirt," I said. "What are you doing here?"

Malori turned around from helping Rhiannon with the dishes. "Rhiannon called and told me you needed some clean clothes."

"So you rushed some right over," I said with a smile. "Thanks, Mal."

"You're welcome," Malori said grinning back at me.

I walked over to Rhiannon, who was busy at the sink, and put my arms around her.

"How long have you been up?" I asked her as I kissed her cheek.

"About an hour," Rhiannon replied, turning to receive a kiss on the lips. "I called Malori and asked her to bring you a change of clothes and decided I needed to clean up the kitchen before you got up."

I looked around the kitchen and noticed it was very neat and tidy. "It looks like you did a great job."

"At least from now on I won't have to do it alone," Rhiannon said.

I gave her a teasing smile and raised my brows. "Really, are you getting a roommate?"

"Brat," she said, batting me lightly on the cheek with the sponge. "As a matter of fact, I think I've found just the right someone. He should be moving his stuff in later today if he knows what's good for him."

"Point taken," I responded with a light laugh.

"That's what I'm here for, favorite brother of mine," Malori informed me, "to give you a ride to Mom and Dad's so you can pick up your car and stuff."

"Is that a fact?" I said. "Does that mean you're taking me to lunch?"

Glancing at the clock on the stove, Malori informed me, "It's closer to supper time. You slept through lunch, lazy-bones."

Wringing out the dishrag, Rhiannon announced, "I'm going to cook you up a home-cooked meal in honor of your first night…" She stopped suddenly. "In honor of our first night together in this house," she said quietly after a moment.

Realizing she'd been about to say "in honor of your first night in my house" before remembering that it was the house I'd bought for Maeve and shared with her for years, I took her hand and pulled her to me.

"This isn't going to be as easy as I thought," Rhiannon said, clinging tightly to me.

Gently stroking her hair, I reassured her. "Honey, we are here, now, and we're together. We go forward from here together." I looked at Malori. "Mal, I think I'll stay here for now and pick up my stuff tomorrow."

"All right, bro," Malori said, "I think that's a good plan. I'll see you two tomorrow."

"Thanks, Malori," Rhiannon said, letting go of me long enough to hug Malori good-bye.

Then it was just Rhiannon and me. We walked to the living room.

"Does the fireplace still work?" I asked her.

"It should," she said.

I got a fire started, and we sat on the floor in front of the couch facing the crackling flames. I held her close to me, and we just sat quietly for a time watching the flames. When she was ready, she began to talk.

"Michael," she said.

"Yes, honey," I replied.

Rhiannon smiled. "I still love it when you call me honey."

Smiling back at her, I said, "I'm glad."

"You do know you are the only man I have ever loved?" Rhiannon asked slowly, with emphasis.

I couldn't imagine that. "I do now," I said.

"You're the only man I've ever been with, Michael," Rhiannon revealed to me.

I didn't know how to respond to that, so I just pulled her closer to me.

"I thought you should know that," she said snuggling even closer. Again we were quiet for a while.

I thought about all the history between us, my history in that house.

"Honey," I said.

She breathed a pleased sigh, "Yes."

"We can't stay here," I told her.

"I know," she said. She'd been thinking the same thing it seemed.

"I've been looking at a place in the islands," I said, "on Saint Thomas."

She was thoughtful for a minute before she said, "I think that would be nice. How soon can we leave?"

"Tomorrow," I said. I couldn't think of any reason we couldn't leave right way.

She turned to look at me. "Just like that?" she asked.

"Just like that," I told her. "If that's what you want."

Rhiannon shook her head, smiling sadly. "What about the

house, and my job?"

"My dad will take care of the house," I assured her. "I'm sure your bosses would understand."

She sat up, and her brow furrowed as she thought about that. "I should give them two weeks' notice, don't you think?"

"Do you really want to wait two weeks?" I asked her.

Rhiannon smiled and shook her head. "No, not really," she admitted. "Can we really leave tomorrow?"

"Just let me make a couple of calls and in a couple of days we'll be on *Cuarto* sailing the Islands," I promised her.

She thought about that a minute, maybe less.

"Make the calls, Michael," Rhiannon said with a smile. "Make the calls."

The first call was to my dad to explain the situation. Then I called the airport to make sure the Seneca would be ready. I checked with Rhiannon to make sure her passport was up to date.

With the planning, packing, and arrangements, it was actually two days later before Rhiannon and I went wheels-up at Wilmington International on our way to Saint Thomas and the marina where I had left *Cuarto*.

We had to make stops in Nassau and the Turks and Caicos on the way but finally arrived and boarded. I'd contacted the folks at the marina to let them know I was returning, and they had her all ready for us.

After we'd stowed our gear, Rhiannon changed into a bikini and laid out a towel on the foredeck. I joined her after double checking that all the hookups were secure and working.

"Are we really here, Michael, or am I going to wake up and find this is all a dream?" Rhiannon asked me.

"We are really here, honey," I assured her.

"I love it when you call me honey," Rhiannon said.

Rhiannon and I spent the next several months sailing around the islands. The calendar showed that summer had passed and fall was upon us, but there among the islands we hardly noticed the change of seasons. As October became November we started thinking about going home for the holidays.

"Could we go for Thanksgiving and stay right through New Year's?" Rhiannon asked me when we began discussing it.

"We could if that's what you wanted to do," I told her.

"I think I'd like to do that," she said.

"We'd need a place to stay," I informed her. "My father found a buyer for the Nadeau house."

"He did?" Rhiannon said, sounding a bit disappointed. "So where would we stay?"

"How would you feel about living in a suite at the Wright Isle Resort for a couple of months?" I asked her.

"Are you serious?" Rhiannon said, before she remembered. "Oh, yeah, you own a big chunk of that place, don't you?"

"As a matter of fact, I do," I acknowledged. "I've already contacted Hernando. Did you know he's planning to retire next spring?"

"Hernando retire?" Rhiannon said. "How will they manage without him?"

"I don't know," I said. "I hope he's been bringing someone along to take over for him."

"Do you think we could stay in the suite we had Prom night?" Rhiannon asked with a grin.

"I think it's been remodeled a couple of times since then, but yes, I think we could," I told her. "Actually, honey, that's the room I asked Hernando to reserve for us."

"I still love it when you call me honey," Rhiannon said. "I

should have known you'd think of that."

I smiled and then checked to see that the small package I'd put in my pocket before I came up on deck was still there.

"Rhiannon, how would you feel about going to a big wedding?" I asked innocently.

"Whose wedding, Michael?" Rhiannon asked as she turned toward me. A look of surprise came to her face when she noticed the ring I was holding sparkling in the sunlight.

"Ours," I said.

"Oh, Michael," Rhiannon said as tears started to fill her eyes.

"I was thinking we could make the trip home a long honeymoon," I said.

Rhiannon took the ring and put in on her finger. She looked at it for a long moment as if expecting it to disappear, and then she looked at me.

"Well," she said expectantly.

Realizing what she was waiting for, I took her hand and slowly got down on one knee.

"Rhiannon, it wasn't that long ago that I thought I could never love again. If not for you, I may never have been able to. You are such a part of me that I don't think I could live without you. Rhiannon, my friend and my lover, will you become my wife?"

Rhiannon's tears streamed, and she was literally shaking as she replied.

"Michael, I thought I had lost you forever. Then, when you lost Maeve, I begged God to take me instead and give her back to you. I loved you so much, and I couldn't bear to see you suffer so."

Rhiannon stopped a minute to collect herself. I felt a lump rising in my throat and tears filling my eyes.

"I have never loved any man but you, Michael, and I

threw that away once. But I promised you that I would always be there for you if you needed me. Now I have another chance and, mister, you can bet your life I'm not throwing this one away. Yes, Michael, I will marry you."

I stood slowly, and with tears rolling down my cheeks, took Rhiannon into my arms and held her. Brushing her hair back from her face, I kissed her warmly and gently and told her I loved her. She wiped at my tears and told me she loved me, too. We kissed again and, without another word between us, went below to our cabin.

About the Author

DW Davis graduated from Western New England College with an accounting degree, after a four year hitch in the Army, and is currently working as a middle school math teacher. DW grew up in coastal North Carolina and still resides in the state's Coastal Plains region with his lovely wife and two sons. *DREAMS ADRIFT* is the third book in the River Dream series.

Connect with DW Davis Online:

On his web site:
http://www.riversailorliterary.com

On Facebook:
http://www.facebook.com/RiverSailorLiterary

On Twitter:
http://twitter.com/DWDavisRSL

www.ingramcontent.com/pod-product-compliance
Lightning Source LLC
Chambersburg PA
CBHW071147170626
46809CB00002B/809